WORD of MOUSE

JAMES PATTERSON is the internationally bestselling author of the highly praised Middle School books, *Homeroom Diaries*, *Kenny Wright: Superhero*, *Jacky Ha-Ha* and the I Funny, Treasure Hunters, House of Robots, Confessions, Maximum Ride, Witch & Wizard and Daniel X series. James Patterson has been the most borrowed author in UK libraries for the past ten years in a row and his books have sold more than 325 million copies worldwide, making him one of the biggest-selling authors of all time. He lives in Florida.

HOW I SURVIVED BULLIES, BROCCOLI, AND SNAKE HILL
(with Chris Tebbetts)

I'm excited for a fun summer at camp—until I find out it's a summer *school* camp. There's no fun and games here, I have a bunk mate called Booger Eater (it's pretty self-explanatory), and we're up against the kids from the "Cool Cabin"… there's gonna be a whole lotta trouble!

ULTIMATE SHOWDOWN
(with Julia Bergen)

Who would have thought that we—Rafe and Georgia—would ever agree on anything? That's right—we're writing a book together. Discover: Who has the best advice on BULLIES? Who's got all the right DANCE MOVES? Who's the cleverest Khatchadorian in town? And the best part? We want you to be part of the fun too!

SAVE RAFE!
(with Chris Tebbetts)

I'm in worse trouble than ever! I need to survive a gut-bustingly impossible outdoor excursion so I can return to school next year. Watch me as I become "buddies" with the scariest girl on the planet, raft down the rapids on a deadly river, and ultimately learn the most important lesson of my life.

JUST MY ROTTEN LUCK
(with Chris Tebbetts)

I'm heading back to the place it all began: Hills Village Middle School, but only if I take "special" classes… If that wasn't bad enough, when I somehow land a place on the school football team, I find myself playing alongside none other than the biggest bully in school, Miller the Killer!

DOG'S BEST FRIEND
(with Chris Tebbetts)
It's a dog-eat-dog world. When I start my own dog-walking empire, I didn't think it could go so horribly wrong! Somehow, I always seem to end up in deep doo-doo...

ESCAPE TO AUSTRALIA
(with Martin Chatterton)
I just won an all-expenses-paid trip of a lifetime to Australia. But here's the bad news: I MIGHT NOT MAKE IT OUT ALIVE!

THE
I FUNNY
SERIES

I FUNNY
(with Chris Grabenstein)
Join Jamie Grimm at middle school where he's on an unforgettable mission to win the Planet's Funniest Kid Comic Contest. Dealing with the school bully (who he also happens to live with) and coping with a disability are no trouble for Jamie when he has laughter on his side.

I EVEN FUNNIER
(with Chris Grabenstein)
Jamie's one step closer to achieving his dream!
This time, be amazed as he fends off the attention of thousands of star-struck girls, watch in awe as he reduces the school bully to a quivering mess, and join the masses as he becomes the most popular kid in school.
Or something like that...

I TOTALLY FUNNIEST
(with Chris Grabenstein)
Jamie's heading to Hollywood for his biggest challenge yet. There's only the small matter of the national finals and eight other laugh-a-minute competitors between him and the trophy—oh, and a hurricane!

I FUNNY TV
(with Chris Grabenstein)

Jamie has achieved his dream of becoming the Planet's Funniest Kid Comic, and now the sky's the limit! Enter a couple of TV executives with an offer for Jamie to star in his very own show...

SCHOOL OF LAUGHS
(with Chris Grabenstein)

Jamie has a national contest trophy and a TV show under his belt, but teaching other kids how to be funny is the toughest gig that he has ever had. And if he fails, his school library will be shut down for good!

The TREASURE HUNTERS series

TREASURE HUNTERS
(with Chris Grabenstein)

The Kidds are not your normal family, traveling the world on crazy adventures to recover lost treasure. But when their parents disappear, Bick and his brothers and sisters are thrown into the biggest (and most dangerous) treasure hunt of their lives. Evil pirates, tough guys and gangsters stand in their way, but can they work together to find mom and dad?

DANGER DOWN THE NILE
(with Chris Grabenstein)

Bick, Beck, Storm and Tommy are navigating their way down the Nile, from a hot and dusty Cairo to deep dark jungles, past some seriously bad guys along the way.

SECRET OF THE FORBIDDEN CITY
(with Chris Grabenstein)
The Kidds are desperately trying to secure the ancient
Chinese artefact that will buy their mother's freedom from
kidnapping pirates.

PERIL AT THE TOP OF THE WORLD
(with Chris Grabenstein)
When the biggest heist in history takes place in Moscow, the
Kidds rush in to save the day—but instead, they're accused of
being the thieves themselves!

HOUSE OF ROBOTS
(with Chris Grabenstein)
Sammy is just your average kid... except he lives in a
house full of robots! Most of the time it's pretty cool. But then
there's E, the worst robot ever. He's a know-it-all, thinks he's
Sammy's brother, AND he's about to go to the same school!
Come see if Sammy *ever* manages to make any friends with
a loser robot tagging along...

ROBOTS GO WILD!
(with Chris Grabenstein)
Sammy and E are finally making some friends at school.
But disaster strikes when E malfunctions just in time to be
upstaged by the super-cool new robot on the block.

ROBOT REVOLUTION
(with Chris Grabenstein)
When Sammy's inventor mom becomes distracted by a
top-secret project, the robots soon begin to fall into disrepair.
Cue a robot revolution!

(with Chris Tebbetts)
Kenny is the life-saving, world-famous superhero
otherwise known as Stainlezz Steel. He's taken down
General Zod twice, beaten Darth Vader at chess… and lives
with his grandma. Ok, sometimes he gets a bit carried away.
But G-ma really does need his help now—and he's going to
have to be a superhero to save the day.

JACKY HA-HA
(with Chris Grabenstein)
With her irresistable urge to tell a joke in every
situation—even when she really shouldn't—twelve-year-
old Jacky Ha-Ha loves to make people laugh. And cracking
wise helps distract her from thinking about not-so-funny
things in her life, like her mom serving in a dangerous,
faraway war, and a dad who's hardly ever home.

WORD of MOUSE

JAMES PATTERSON
AND CHRIS GRABENSTEIN

ILLUSTRATED BY JOE SUTPHIN

1 3 5 7 9 10 8 6 4 2

Young Arrow
20 Vauxhall Bridge Road
London SW1V 2SA

Young Arrow is part of the Penguin Random House group of companies
whose addresses can be found at global.penguinrandomhouse.com

Penguin
Random House
UK

First published by Young Arrow in 2016
First published in paperback by Young Arrow in 2017

www.penguin.co.uk

A CIP catalogue record for this book is available from the British Library

ISBN 9781784754228

Printed and bound by in Great Britain by Clays Ltd, St Ives Plc

Penguin Random House is committed to a sustainable future for
our business, our readers and our planet. This book is made
from Forest Stewardship Council® certified paper.

For Red Boy
—JP

For Parker, Tiger Lilly,
and Phoebe Squeak
—CG

CHAPTER 1

*"The world is always biggest
when you're small."*
—**Isaiah**

M y story starts on the day I lost my entire family.
    I'm running as fast as I can behind my big
brothers and sisters. Down the hall. Past the mop
bucket. Toward the open door.

We're escaping from a place that's foul and creepy
and 100 percent HORRIBLE!

It's also the only home my family and I have ever
known.

My brothers and sisters are leading the way to our
freedom. All ninety-six of 'em. I'm the youngest, not
to mention the smallest. All I have to do is tail after
them, just like I always do. Wherever they lead, I will

follow. I know it'll be a safer place. And better. It has to be!

Abe says so. Winnie, too.

We squeeze through that tiny crack between the door and the wall and enter the Land of the Giants.

Outside.

The place none of us has ever been before.

Have I mentioned how terrified I am?

Oh, no!

A lumpy black mountain reeking of rancid vegetables blocks our way forward. It forces my family to split up. To scatter in all directions.

"You guys?" I cry. "Wait up!"

They can't wait. It's too dangerous.

I try taking a shortcut to catch up with them. I run *over* the mountain.

Bad idea.

My right rear paw punches through something as thin as an eggshell. My leg plunges down into a slimy hole, and I can't lift it out. This isn't a mountain. It's a big, black plastic sack filled with garbage.

"You guys?"

My brothers and sisters have totally disappeared.

And I'm trapped.

So, I do what I always do. I panic.

"HELP!" I yell.

This escape was my big brother Benji's idea. But Benji's gone. So are Abe and Winnie and—

I hear the heavy thuds of human shoes behind me. Someone's coming.

I yank at my leg. It won't budge. I yank again.

On the third yank, I finally tug my foot free. I need to run. I need to find my family. Because without them, I don't have any idea where I'm supposed to go or what I'm supposed to do!

On the other side of the garbage mountain, I skirt around a crumpled bag labeled D-O-R-I-T-O-S and reach a ledge.

"Winnie? Abe?"

I look around. Can't see anybody.

Then I look down.

There's a three-foot drop to a steel grate covering a dark tunnel.

I close my eyes tight and leap.

I land with a splash in cold, scummy water. I hate when my feet get wet.

"You guys?" I call out. "Did anybody else take the sewer drain? Anybody? Hello?"

No answer. Not even a squeak. Just my own voice echoing back at me.

I've heard humans say, "Are you a man, or are you a mouse?" when one of them is afraid and the other one needs him to be brave.

Well, I am definitely a mouse.

My name is Isaiah. I have never been more frightened in my whole life, and that's saying something, because my whole life has been one big fright fest. But it doesn't get any worse than this.

I don't know where I am. And I've lost my family. Or they lost me.

Either way, for the first time in my life, I'm completely alone.

CHAPTER 2

**"God gave us the acorns,
but He doesn't crack them open for us."
—Isaiah**

I hear a siren.

Flashes of red light slice through the darkness, along with the shrieks of a siren. *Yipes!* Someone just sounded the alarm.

I want to hide forever in the darkest corner of this dripping drain, but something inside me says, *Keep running, Isaiah. Never let them catch you! Go find your family! Hurry! Move it or lose it!*

I scamper deeper into the darkness.

I'm extremely speedy. It's all those months I spent on the exercise wheel. Swinging out my tail for balance, I round a blind curve. The strobing flashes of red disappear. So does all the other light. I use my whiskers, just like Mom taught me before she disappeared from the Horrible Place, to feel my way along the damp walls. I barrel headfirst into a black tunnel of nothingness.

And my feet keep getting wetter.

Suddenly, up ahead, I see a split shaft of light.

It's another storm drain.

I scuttle up the slick side wall and come out in an alley littered with trash, some of which looks pretty tasty. But when you're a mouse on the run, trying to catch up with the rest of your family, you really can't stop for a snack, no matter how tempting. I slip on a squishy brown banana peel, slide sideways toward a pile of boxes, and skid through an opening skinnier than a page in a book.

When I glide out (on my bottom) on the other side, I hear voices.

Human voices.

"Find them, you idiot!" snarls one. "Find them all!"

"This isn't my fault," blubbers the other. "I only left the ding-dang door open for a second."

I don't wait to hear any more.

I scale the side of a building. Climb straight up

it using tiny holes that humans wouldn't even know were there. When I reach the top, I see a thick, black utility line swaying in the breeze. I spring off the wall, fly through the air, and land with a *boing* and a bounce.

Using my tail for balance, the way a tightrope walker uses a pole, I race along the bobbing wire.

Soon I'm over another alley. Or maybe a toxic waste dump. The air smells so extremely gross, it makes my whiskers quiver. Rust. Putrid chemicals. The scent of rotting eggs.

My ears are blasted by the shrieks of that alarm horn. It makes my spine shiver all the way down to the tip of my tail. I need my brothers and sisters to buck me up and make me brave.

But I still can't see any of them.

I shout down to the ground anyway.

"You guys? Abe? Winnie? Anybody? *Where are you?*"

CHAPTER 3

"A mouse may run swiftly,
but it can never escape its own tail."
—Isaiah

I feel like I've been running for hours, even though it's probably been only five minutes.

The humans are far behind me now, but they're loud—and my ears are extremely sensitive.

"That's ninety-five," says one.

"Make that ninety-six," says the other. "Gotcha!"

Oh, no! They caught my whole family. Abe and Winnie and Benji and—

"Good work," cries one of the humans. "Who's missing?"

"One of the ding-dang blue ones. The runt."

"That's Blue 97. Look! Something's moving behind that barrel!"

"You ain't gettin' away, Blue Boy!"

They take off. So do I.

From the fading sound of their voices, I'd say we're heading in opposite directions.

Have you ever been separated from your family in a strange place?

What did you do? Sit down and cry your eyes out? That's my plan, too.

The terrible thing is, I know exactly where they are. Somewhere I can never, ever go back to.

I know the others will try to escape again. My big brother Benji isn't a quitter. He won't ever give up. He'll hatch another scheme. Soon.

But until then, what would I do? Live in the outside all by myself? I've never had to find my own food or a place to sleep before. Where would I even start?

All of a sudden, the clouds part. The midday sun warms my fur and dries my toes.

I decide to keep moving. I need to find a place where I can hide until Benji and the rest of my family try to break out of the Horrible Place again. When they do, I'll be waiting for 'em!

Now, I know what you're probably thinking: "Wait a second, Isaiah. You're a mouse. Mice are supposed to be nocturnal creatures, nearly blind. That much noontime sunshine must really hurt your eyeballs."

Well, first off, if you don't mind, we mice are nocturnal *and* crepuscular, which, of course, means we're active throughout the night, as well as at dusk and dawn. How do I know a big word like *crepuscular?* Oh, I know all sorts of big words. For instance, *tenebrous.* It's another word for crepuscular.

But as far as the sunshine frying my eyes, not to worry. Unlike a lot of garden-variety field mice, day or night, I have practically perfect eyesight. My sense of smell is amazing, too. Ten times better than a dog's. In fact, I'm incredibly different in a lot of different ways.

For instance, if you saw me, you would definitely scream. Not just because I'm a mouse, but because I'm a *blue* mouse. The same bright sky blue as the marshmallow rabbits the Long Coats were nibbling on last Easter.

Not to brag, but I'm also very smart, with a very advanced (dare I say *urbane?*) vocabulary for an animal who only weighs one ounce and measures five and a half inches long.

All of my brothers and sisters are special, too, but in different ways. And we're not all blue. Winnie, for instance, is chartreuse—a bright shade of yellow-green. Abe? He's red, or, as he calls it, "electric crimson."

I'm guessing, however, that none of my ninety-six siblings are as stupendously scared as I am right now, because, basically, I'm the coward in the family. It's true. Out of all ninety-seven of us, I'm the biggest scaredy-cat.

Yipes!

See? I just scared myself with the word *cat*.

Oh, no, I said it again! My legs go all rubbery as I run full speed along the power line. I slip off and tumble down, head over tail!

There's no net, but luckily, there *is* a pile of soft, fluffy leaves.

I know what you're thinking. I'm not proud of my faintheartedness and timidity, but it's a sad fact. Benji once said my fur should be yellow instead of blue.

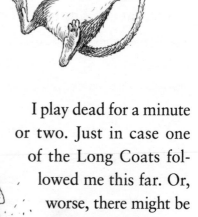

I play dead for a minute or two. Just in case one of the Long Coats followed me this far. Or, worse, there might be a bird circling overhead, looking for lunch.

When all I can hear is the wind rustling through the tall grass and the thumping of my own heart, I slowly raise my head and, hoping against hope, scan the horizon. I'm looking for a familiar snout. A friendly set of whiskers.

"Abe?" I whimper. "Winnie? Benji?"

Of course there's no answer. What I heard the humans say is true. They've all been caught. Every last one.

Except me. The most cowardly mouse in my whole family.

CHAPTER 4

**"When you've already lost everything,
you have nothing left to lose."**
—Isaiah

I stand up on my hind legs and check out my surroundings.

I'm alone in the world. And I have absolutely no idea where in the world I am.

I figure I have a choice:

A) I could turn around, run back to the Horrible Place, and turn myself in to the Long Coats. If I do that, I'll be with my family again, sucking sugar water out of a tube and munching on kibble before nightfall, all snug and toasty in my bed of cedar shavings.

B) I can keep running. Find someplace to hide.
Wait for my family to escape and find me.

I go with B. Right before we ran out the back door, my cedar shavings got sort of soggy. Don't tell anybody, but the idea of escaping the Horrible Place was such a terrifying thought, I wet my bed.

I read somewhere (yes, I can *read*—how'd you think I learned all those big words?) that "we have nothing to fear but fear itself."

Okay, a human definitely wrote that. We mice are so small we have plenty to be afraid of. Birds, cats, and clumsy mop pushers who wear clunky work boots.

I may not be courageous, but I am definitely curious. For instance, I wonder what's beyond the tree line at the far side of this field I just landed in?

So I scamper across the tall grass (it tickles) and scurry through a thick stand of evergreens, and just like that, I'm in the suburbs. I think. I can't be certain because I've never seen the Land of Suburbia before. I've only read about it.

That's the one good thing I can say about the Horrible Place: we had books. Lots and lots of books.

A whole library full of 'em. We also had tests. Lots and lots of tests.

But, sometimes, when the Long Coats weren't looking, I'd read for fun. I liked adventure stories. In fact, I always wanted to go on a Grand Adventure. Now I know it's just another way to say you're lost and on your own.

Still, there's that niggling curiosity.

The world I just entered is so different from anything I've ever known.

I wander around and check out the sights. Lots of trees, parked cars, and abandoned tricycles. I stick pretty close to the curbs and gutters, just in case I have to make another emergency storm-drain exit.

Some of the big windows in the giant human houses have cats in them. I know they know I'm out here. Cats are clever. Especially when they're hungry.

Speaking of which...

After all of my running and jumping and trembling with fear, the sugar water I gulped down for breakfast (I was too nervous to even look at my kibble) has totally evaporated. I start nosing around for something to eat. And I'm not being too picky or particular.

Did you know that the word *mouse* supposedly came from the Sanskrit word *mus,* which means *thief?* Now, I don't typically think of myself as a thief. I've never taken anything that wasn't freely given to me. I never had to.

But scurrying through Suburbia, a stranger in a strange land, I realize I might not have much of a choice. No Long Coat is going to come along and toss me my daily scoop of crunchy kibble.

Fortunately, a lot of these human homes have large wheeled bins parked in the grass just above the curb. They're all very fragrant.

I sniff the air at the base of one of these tall plastic towers. I can't believe my luck. It's a rolling silo stuffed with slightly used food. Using my claws like grappling hooks, I scale the sheer cliff of Mount Breakfast Buffet and perch atop its summit. One of the white plastic bags stuffed inside the enormous bin is open at the top. I see grapes. A slice of bread speckled with blue-green blotches. And some lumpy mush that might be mashed potatoes (I read about that in a cookbook).

It's a smorgasbord!

My stomach gurgles to remind me that I'm starving

and to urge me to steal anything that's edible. Yes, for the first time in my short life, I am acting like a true mouse (or a *mus*). I'm a food thief.

And I'm loving it!

This gently used food is delicious!

I gobble three wrinkled grapes. Scoop up the mushy stuff (turns out it's cold oatmeal with maple syrup). Devour an apple core.

It's all so scrumptious! I'm discovering new tastes.

Expanding my culinary horizons. Like I said, I was raised on nothing but kibble. Dry, disgusting stuff that tastes like cardboard. How do I know what cardboard tastes like? I just accidentally nibbled the corner of a cereal box and recognized the flavor right away. Kibble.

I'm so glad I didn't turn tail and head back to the Horrible Place. This new world is much more delicious.

I lean back on my soft bread bed to savor yet another wrinkled grape when I feel something nudge my food tower.

Something big.

I peek over the edge.

Yipes!

It's a rat!

CHAPTER 5

**"All of us are given gifts.
How we use them is up to us."**
—Isaiah

My fantastic food fortress is being attacked by rats. Giant, buck-toothed, slimy-skinned, mean-tempered RATS!

Yes, rats are related to mice. We're both members of the rodent family. But rats are like the greedy, violent, and despicable cousins. I don't mean to disparage my own extended family, but come on, let's be honest here: rats are awful.

I feel a double thump down below. I muster enough courage to take another peek over the edge of my food barrel.

Yipes.

I do not like what I see.

A gang of huge rats is streaming up out of the nearest sewer drain.

Obviously, the rats smelled the deliciousness of the Slightly Used Food Silo just like I did. Now they want to knock my rolling food cart over and gobble up all the grub that spills out of it—and then nibble on *me* for dessert.

Good thing the barrel I chose to dive into has wheels. When the rats nudge its base, it doesn't topple over. It simply scoots sideways in the grass.

23

Frustrated, the rats grumble and bash into the base of the bin even harder, using their heads as battering rams. That's okay. They don't use their heads for much else.

You see, my ratty cousins may be huge and ugly, but they're also dumb. Then again, they haven't been given the "educational opportunities" that I have. None of them is familiar with the theories of balance and weight shift.

On the other hand, they are smart enough to have me trapped. No way am I leaping down to become a bite-sized rat snack.

The crazy rodents keep bumping and thumping and shoving the barrel sideways. The leader of the rat pack looks up and sees me. He twitches his whiskers and sniggers. It is not a friendly sound. It's more like he's smacking his lips in anticipation of the mousy mousse to come.

So I decide it's time to display another one of my rare and unusual talents. There's more to me than just being blue. I take in a deep breath and rise up to my full height, which, just to remind you, is less than six inches.

Compared to me, the rats are gigantic. As big as work boots. It doesn't matter. Like I said, I have this pretty incredible thing I can do.

"KIBBLE!" I scream.

That's right. I can make sounds beyond the usual mouse squeaks and peeps.

I have a *voice*. I can actually speak some human words, especially ones I've heard over and over.

"KIBBLE!" I shout.

The top rat looks up at me with a new expression in his beady little eyes. I recognize the look. It's fear.

"KIBBLE!" This time I wave my paws like I'm some sort of mad, demented boogeymouse.

Top Rat shrieks and, with a whip of his wiry tail, races back to his sewer grate. The rest of his rat buddies skitter off behind him.

In a flash, they're gone.

And my heart wants to explode inside my chest. It was the first time I've had to save my own life!

I might've scared off the rats, but I'm still pretty scared myself. Okay, I'm petrified. Rat attacks will do that to you.

I want my family!

By the way, did you know that, like most mice mothers, mine had all *ninety-seven* of us in less than a year? Why so many children? you wonder. Well, the Long Coats say that the average mouse only lives a year, maybe two. I guess we need a lot of new kids or else our whole species could go the way of the dinosaurs and disappear from the face of the Earth.

But I also heard one of the Long Coats say that all the mice from the Horrible Place are different from the average mouse in every way imaginable. One even said I might live as long as a human being!

How long is that? Humans, because they never have to worry about birds or cats or being stepped on (or being eaten by their stupid rat cousins), can live much, much longer than mice.

Wouldn't that be amazing?

Think of all the birthday parties I would have!

CHAPTER 6

*"Be careful.
That light at the end of the tunnel
could be an oncoming train."*
—Isaiah

When I'm absolutely, positively, unquestionably certain that the rats are gone, I grab a hunk of green bread for the road and hop out of my food barrel.

I need to keep moving. I dash down to the street and, staying close to the concrete curb, follow the road to wherever it might lead.

Yipes!

I didn't want it to lead to *this*. Because this is worse than all those deranged rodents ramming my food barrel.

This is a cat.

It's slinking around. Slow and cool. Searching for the best angle of attack. Its shoulders sway easily as it circles me, just like a lion, which, by the way, is just a huge window cat without the litter box. All cats are excellent hunters. That's *their* super special talent.

Frozen in fear, I have time to study this particular beast. It's a black sphynx cat. Did you know that sphynx cats are hairless? They're also very muscular, with extremely powerful necks and paw pads so thick they look like they're walking on pillows.

Yes, I know a lot about cats. I also know I am in a life-or-death situation. So, I try my trick again. Maybe it'll save my life twice today.

"KIBBLE!"

The cat cocks its wedge-shaped head. Confusion fills its evil, acid-yellow eyes.

I seize my moment and dash up the driveway. Unfortunately, the wrinkled, hairless monster chases after me.

I dive for the shrubbery under the porch. The cat dives after me.

I dodge right, aiming for the corner where the porch meets the steps.

The cat mirrors my every move, blocking my escape. I'm trapped, with my back up against the bricks.

But the cat doesn't pounce.

It wants to play. A game called Cat and Mouse, which, in my humble opinion, should be renamed Worst Game Ever. It's like Ping-Pong, only I'm the ball and the cat's deadly paws are the paddles.

As if it can hear my thoughts, the cat flicks its massive paw and I go flying against the wall.

Ow.

When I bounce back, he bops me again with his other giant mitt. He's loving this. He even giggles a hideously hissy "heh-heh-heh." And then he whacks me against the wall again.

I'm seeing stars twinkling behind my eyes.

The cat creeps closer. So close, I can read its name tag.

How adorable.

His name is Lucifer.

CHAPTER 7

*"You have to stand for something,
otherwise you'll spend your whole life
on your butt."*
—**Isaiah**

So there I am. Cornered.

And the devil cat is ready for the next round of Whack-A-Mouse.

I decide enough is enough. I have reached my limit, ladies and gentlemen. I am tired of being attacked for who I am. I will not become this cat's furry toy.

I am a mouse, which you'll remember comes from the Sanskrit word *mus*, for *thief*. Therefore, it is time to rob this prune-skinned fiend of his freakish fun.

Lucifer's tag jingles as he winds up his right paw to swat me again. I curl up into an extremely tight ball. Lucifer rears back and smacks me. A real wallop.

I bounce hard off the brick, rebounding like I'm a Super Ball made of compressed rubber. I fly straight at the cat. I smack him, headfirst, right in his gut.

His "meow" becomes a "me-OUCH!"

I drop to the ground. Tuck and roll.

And while Lucifer's clutching his tummy with his front paws, I sink my small but extremely pointy teeth into one of his hind legs. I go for the ankle. Aim for a tender tendon at the back of his heel. A tendon that's easy to see since baldy has no fur.

Lucifer screeches like a hippopotamus just stepped on his tail.

I take off, flying. Not literally (I can't actually fly), but like I said earlier, I am speedy. If you ever get the chance, chase some cheese on a workout wheel. It'll make you fast, especially when you're furious.

Lucifer isn't too keen on chasing me anymore. I glance over my shoulder and see that he's licking his wounds. Literally.

I use my whiskers and tail to chart a course through the flower bed's underbrush. I run along the side of the brick house and scoot around to the backyard.

Is Lucifer chasing after me again? I'm too busy running to look behind me.

Up ahead, I see a stockade fence, made out of wooden planks. There's a tiny hole where a pine knot used to be. A hole Lucifer couldn't fit through in a million years.

I make a break for it.

I sprint across the grass, take a flying leap, stretch out my legs, and soar through the knothole. I am actually flying! (Well, sort of.)

I shoot through the hole and land on the other side of the fence in a bed of pine-bark mulch beneath a row of fruit trees. There's an overly ripe apple lying on the ground. I munch my way around it while I contemplate my next move. With cruel cats and hungry birds on the hunt, it just isn't safe for a bright blue mouse to wander around outdoors.

The apple trees are behind a house that looks a lot like the one where I met Lucifer. Actually, a lot of homes in Suburbia look the same.

I wipe the apple juice off my paws, fluff up my fur, and head toward the house.

And hope this one doesn't have a cat.

CHAPTER 8

*"No matter the temperature,
home is always colder
when there's no family to share it with."*
—Isaiah

Maybe I should've kept on running.

Maybe I should've found another storm drain to hide in.

Maybe I should've crawled back to the Horrible Place to be with my family again.

Instead, I move closer to the house because I can't resist the tantalizing aroma of cinnamon, apples, butter, and brown sugar wafting out of its screen door. I recognize that scent. It's fresh-baked apple pie!

One day, not too many sunrises ago, a Long Coat brought an apple pie to the Horrible Place. She walked right past me with a cardboard box all tied up with red and white string. I was working out on the wheel, but the scent stopped me dead in my tracks. In my humble opinion, apple pie smells just like heaven.

I study the screen door of the house. There's a flap set into it, with "Pet Door" printed on the rubber strip edging the fabric. That means the flap is a door designed for friendly animals to use as an entrance and exit.

I've always considered myself to be the friendly sort. So, I bound up the short set of steps and poke my head through the pet door.

Mmm! My whiskers twitch with delight at the strong scent of apple pie goodness. I climb through the pet door. I'm inside the house.

So is the apple pie baker.

She's a large woman in a flour-dusted apron. She has her hands on her hips and is scowling down at me. She also has a rolling pin.

"Get out of my kitchen, you filthy rodent!" she screams.

She flings her rolling pin at me. I take that as my cue to skedaddle. I dive back through the pet door and scamper away.

"And stay out, vermin!"

Her words hurt as they echo in my ears. Vermin is not a very nice thing to call any creature. It means you're a pest or a parasite. A bug to be squashed. A fly to be swatted. A mouse to be trapped in a sticky glue box.

Yes, I not only understand words, I also understand their meaning. Sometimes I wish I wasn't so "gifted and talented."

Just between you and me, I don't really enjoy knowing that there are people in the world who hate me even though they don't even know me.

So I keep running.

But soon I'm slowing down. Okay, I'm walking. Even all that cheese-chasing on the exercise wheel couldn't give you the stamina you need to run for eight hours straight.

The streets are dark except for one or two pools of light underneath the lonely street lamps.

More time passes. Stars sparkle like broken icicles in the sky. I realize I'm shivering. For once, it's not because I'm afraid. No, my teeth are chattering because I'm cold.

Usually, mice stay warm by cuddling together in

a burrow and sharing body heat. Tonight, however, that is not an option. I'm alone. I'm also exhausted. I take a chance and sneak up on the least intimidating home I can find. The bottom is made of cinder blocks, which have hollow spaces inside them, just like snug concrete burrows. I notice an opening in a cinder block with clumps of old, dry leaves and pine needles. I find some velvety green moss growing on a rock, scrape it off, and wrap it in a waxy leaf I pluck off a bush. It will make a nice pillow.

When my home for the night is as comfy as possible, I crawl in and curl up.

I'm pretty cozy. I'm also pretty lonely. I've never spent a night away from my family before. As horrible as the Horrible Place was, at least we were all together. I miss my brothers and sisters.

Abe, Benji, Clement, Delilah, Eli, Felicity, Felix...

In my head, I recite all their names. When I hit Zuzu, I start all over again. On the third pass, I fall asleep, dreading the dreams that might come.

The craziest day of my life has turned into the saddest night of my life.

And I don't expect tomorrow to be much better.

CHAPTER 9

*"Hunger drives the wolf out of the wood
and the mouse into the garbage can."*
—Isaiah

Most mice usually sleep about twelve hours a day. When I wake up, I feel like I may have slept for an entire day. Maybe longer. I remember waking up once, fluffing up my moss pillow, and covering my eyes with a clump of straw when a dusty sunbeam found its way into my burrow and tried to warm my face.

I ignored it and went back to sleep.

But the second time the sun bursts through my thimble-sized doorway, my stomach won't let me cover up my eyes and roll over. It's growling angrily for me to feed it.

Get up, Isaiah, I tell myself. *No one's coming with your morning scoop of kibble. If you want to eat, you need to go out there and find yourself some food!*

I crawl out of my nest in the wall. My plan is to return to the sidewalks of Suburbia and find another rolling food tower. I scamper across the front lawn, aiming for another Used Food Bin conveniently parked near the curb.

Suddenly, there is a tremendous noise. Air explodes. A monster grinds its teeth. The whole earth shakes.

A hulking white truck rumbles slowly up the street with a human hanging off the back.

I duck behind a ceramic lawn ornament to hide.

Peeking around the plaster burro pulling a donkey cart filled with potted petunias, I spy a burly human in a shiny orange vest scooping up my breakfast buffet and dumping it into the wide-open jaws at the rear of the mammoth white truck.

This is horrible! I'm being out-*mus*ed. They're stealing the food I was going to steal, and there's nothing I can do about it.

When they're finished feeding the back end of the

truck *my* breakfast, the humans toss the rolling barrel on its side in the strip of grass between the sidewalk and the curb. Then they rumble down the road to plunder the next bin.

I look up the street to where they've already been. All the barrels are lying on their sides. I know they're empty. My delicious breakfast has been fed to the giant white truck, which, it seems, is even hungrier than I am. The humans are feeding it every bin they can find on the block.

Is this what it means to truly be a mouse? Is my life outside of the Horrible Place doomed to become nothing but an endless quest for food and shelter?

When the humans and their hungry truck are two houses away, I sneak up to the empty barrel.

I smell something foul.

I see a puddle of wet, chunky slop trapped in one of the dimpled indentations near the barrel's bottom. The soupy stew smells ripe, rank, and rotten.

But, it *is* food.

I hold my nose and lap it up.

Yes, being a mouse—even one with bright blue fur—isn't pretty.

Neither is the food.

CHAPTER 10

**"Hope is putting faith to work
when giving up would be easier."
—Isaiah**

I'm choking down a chunk of mystery meat.

Or it could be a bit of underdone potato. It's covered in so much spoiled, greasy gravy, it's hard to say.

My stomach lurches. The vinegary smell is triggering my gag reflex. I feel like a cat hacking up a hairball as I spit out the mealy glob.

Come on, Isaiah, I tell myself. *Beggars can't be choosers.*

Yes, we can, says the little voice in my head that doesn't want to suck down any more disgusting slop.

How about finding food the old-fashioned way, like gathering nuts and berries?

Where are we going to find nuts and berries? I ask myself.

We could try talking to the squirrels, suggests the little voice. *They're sort of mouse-ish and seem friendlier than rats...*

Suddenly, I hear something that silences my internal debate.

My food barrel is catching a faraway sound—a song—and amplifying it until it surrounds me. Suddenly, this garbage can has become a symphony hall.

The singer's voice is beautiful. Absolutely incredible.

An angelic soprano singing a lilting melody very similar to the lullaby my mother used to croon right after I was born.

It's the song of a mouse.

Oh, yes, it's true. Mice can sing. We're some of the very few mammals who can carry a tune—whales, bats, humans, and mice. In fact, we use the same part of our brain to serenade each other as humans do. Mice also get goosebumps, like the tingly ones I have now from listening to the sweet singing. We have

45

so much in common with people, you'd think they'd treat us better.

But I don't want to dwell on that right now. I don't even want to think about it.

I just want to rest here for a moment and listen to this lovely love song. Because that's what it is. Usually, boy mice sing love ballads to attract girl mice. But *this* song is being sung by a girl. I can tell. Of course, she isn't singing it for me. How could she? We haven't even met.

Yet.

Forget food. I must seek out and find this mid-morning nightingale.

I march out of the trash barrel with renewed determination. There are mice in Suburbia. *Singing mice,* at that. Now I don't feel so alone in the world anymore—I simply have to find this musical mouse! She must be nice to sing so delightfully.

I roll in some fragrant clover to wipe the garbage juice off my body. I nibble some grass because it has chlorophyll (that's what makes it green), and chlorophyll is excellent for battling bad breath. I want to look and smell my best when I meet this magnificent melody maker.

I also grab a pretty yellow dandelion. It's only right that I bring her flowers. I'm a huge fan.

I perk up my ears. Listen for her voice. Follow her song.

Because wherever it leads, that's where I want to be.

CHAPTER 11

"What sunshine is to flowers,
smiles are to a mouse."
—Isaiah

Well, hidey-ho!
Not only does the girl mouse have a beautiful voice, she also has a be-YOO-tiful smile and lovely curling eyelashes longer than most whiskers.

Of course, she hasn't seen me yet.

This is probably a good thing. The magnificent songstress is blessed with dark brown fur, the color of rich, hot cocoa. Mine, as you might recall, is blue. Bright, blazing, electric neon blue.

I know the brown-furred beauty will probably stop singing the second she spies my mind-boggling

blueness. After all, it *is* extremely shocking. So, for now, I will simply tarry here in the shrubbery, sniff my dandelion, and listen to her sing to herself and the bees buzzing around the rosebuds. Bees always like to hum along whenever mice sing their songs.

My, what a sweet, dare I say *dulcet*, voice she has. *Dulcet*, of course is another word for *sweet* but I think *dulcet* sounds much more soothing and melodious than *sweet*, so...

50

Uh-oh.

She stopped singing. She's looking around. She senses someone is watching her. All mice are very good at sensing intruders, because it could always be a cat.

I decide to take a chance. I pop out from my hiding place and bow deeply.

"Have no fear, beautiful songstress!" I say.

She yelps anyway. But she doesn't run away, which I take as an encouraging sign.

"It is only I, Isaiah."

"Y-y-you," she stammers, "you're blue."

"Actually, I'm not feeling blue at all. Your singing makes me very happy."

She doesn't appreciate my little quip. Regular mice seldom do. Instead, she points a paw at me.

"Your fur. It's weird."

"Indeed it is. However, I prefer to think of it as 'special.'"

"It's weird."

"Perhaps. However, I know a mouse named Abe with crimson fur. My sister Winnie, on the other hand, is chartreuse."

"What are crimson and chartreuse?"

"Crimson is red. Chartreuse is a color halfway between yellow and green."

"Color?"

Oops. I forgot. Regular mice (not me) are color-blind. All they can see are black, white, and—yes—blue. I must look like a mouse-shaped piece of sky.

"I suppose you've never seen a blue mouse before, living as you do here in the Land of Suburbia…"

Now her brown fur bristles. I see the hackles on her neck shoot straight up. "What's wrong with where I live?"

"Nothing. It's only that—"

"I've been places, you know. I've been next door. And that house over there, too!"

"I'm sure you have. You also have the sweetest, most dulcet singing voice I've ever heard."

"What does *dulcet* mean?"

"Sweet. Like honey."

Now she looks even more upset. "You weren't supposed to listen to me sing."

I can tell she isn't exactly charmed by me so far.

I smile and wiggle my whiskers the way I've seen my big brother Rudolpho do whenever he flirts with girls. "Mademoiselle, how could I possibly resist?"

"Easy. You could walk away."

Which is what she does.

Away from me.

CHAPTER 12

"No mouse's head aches while
he or she comforts another."
—Isaiah

I'm not exactly sure why, but I follow after her.

Probably because I'm tired of being alone, and loneliness is an empty feeling worse than hunger. She is the only soul who hasn't wanted to kill or capture me since I escaped, and I can't just let her go.

"I don't mean to bother you," I call, trying my best to keep up with her. "But, you see, recently I lost my whole family. Of course, you might wonder how that could be possible, for one mouse to lose ninety-six others, but we were fleeing the Horrible Place. It was Benji's idea. Benji's my big brother. Well, one of them. I have forty-eight brothers and—"

Suddenly, the pretty brown mouse stops in her tracks so she can spin around to look at me.

"You lost your mischief?"

I nod sadly.

By the way, a *mischief* is the proper term for a group or family of mice. Like a gaggle of geese, a troop of baboons, a peep of chickens, or a scourge of mosquitos. A mischief of mice!

"But," I add, "I'm quite certain my family will soon escape again and come looking for me. I left something of a scented trail for them to follow. They'll be able to sniff the ground and track me. I have a very distinctive odor."

The girl twitches her whiskers as she inhales the air around me. "You smell like garbage rolled in clover."

I use my front paws to smooth out my matted fur. It's still sort of sticky from all the rotten juice sloshing around at the bottom of that trash barrel.

"Well," I say, "I had a rather unfortunate day yesterday. And, frankly, today hasn't been much better. Actually, it might've been *two* days ago that we fled the Horrible Place. I've lost track of time…"

"Just like you lost your family."

I look down at my feet. Oh, the shame of it all.

"Yes," I mumble. "We were being chased, and I should have stayed with them…"

She softens. Slightly. "My name is Mikayla. My mischief lives in that house over there."

"You have a mischief?"

"Of course I do. And guess what? I haven't lost mine."

I know she's just teasing me, but still, it stings. The truth, I have found, often does.

"What's that thing in your ear?" Mikayla asks.

I touch the tag that was clamped on my ear when I was born. It said 97, which was what the Longcoats called me at the Horrible Place. I would've told them my real name, if they'd bothered to ask.

But all I say is, "I don't want to talk about it." All of my family has ear tags, but none of the mice out here do. It's just another way I'm "weird."

"Tell me, Isaiah," she says, looking me up and down, "when was the last time you had something to eat that didn't come from the bottom of a gar-bage bin?"

I burp up something foul that reminds me of my so-called breakfast. "It's been a while," I admit.

"Well, thanks to the Brophys, we always have plenty of food. It's good stuff, too. And we don't mind sharing," says Mikayla, finally taking pity on me. "Come on. Follow me."

Now it's my turn to be confused. "What are the Brophys?" I ask as we scamper ahead.

"Our human hosts. They're total slobs. They eat in every room of the house. And I mean *every* room, even the one for, you know..."

I nod. I believe she is referring to the laundry room. Or perhaps the living room, which of course, is for living, not eating. I read that human homes have rooms for all sorts of purposes. Dining rooms for dining, bathrooms for baths, and TV rooms for staring at electronic boxes.

"The Brophys make scavenging easy," says Mikayla as we follow a smudge mark along the back wall of the ramshackle rattletrap of a house she had pointed out earlier. The smudge is a buildup of dirt and oil from mouse fur rubbing against the wall. It's like a road sign for a regular route taken by Mikayla's family.

"You're certain the rest of your family won't mind me barging in like this?"

"Not as long as you pull your weight, which shouldn't be too hard because, frankly, Isaiah, you look like you weigh less than a maple leaf."

It seems Mikayla enjoys poking gentle fun at me.

And, to tell you the truth, I don't really mind. It's what family members do with each other.

Wait a second. Mikayla said I need to pull my weight. Is it possible?

Well, hidey-ho and what do you know? Mikayla's not just taking me into her den for a visit. She's inviting me into her mischief!

CHAPTER 13

"Those who give have everything.
Those who don't have nothing at all."
—Isaiah

Wowzers!
And I thought *my* family was big.

Mikayla has more than two hundred brothers, sisters, aunts, uncles, cousins, and second cousins once removed.

Mikayla lets loose with a shrill whistle. It's not as pretty as her singing, but it sure gets folks' attention.

"Everybody!" she shouts. "This is Isaiah. He's sort of an orphan and sort of lost. He has an earring and his fur is blue. Deal with it."

"Welcome, Isaiah," says an old mouse who, I'm guessing, is the grandfather of everybody else huddled in the bustling burrow. "My name is James the Wise. Might I ask you a question?"

"Certainly," I say.

"Why is your fur so...so...*blue?*"

"I'm not certain, sir. It's just always been that way. Blue."

"Welcome, new blue friend," he proclaims. "Your orphan days are behind you. This shall be your new home. Our mischief is your mischief."

The other mice squeak with glee. I do, too! After a night alone in the wild, I am safe in a mischief again.

But then I remember something important.

"Can you be my 'right now' family? My forever family is trapped inside the Horrible Place. But they're all going to escape again, I know it," I say to James with a nervous chuckle, because I don't want to sound ungrateful for the hospitality, which, by the way, we mice are famous for.

Seriously.

Mice will always take in strangers, stragglers, or lost babies. (I think I might be all three.) In fact, we mice would make excellent innkeepers. Except we'd probably scare off all our human guests when we fluffed up their pillows.

"Of course," says James, "until you and your family are reunited, our home is your home."

My stomach makes that gurgly noise again because my nose has picked up the scent of something delicious. Something with chocolate.

"And, uh, don't mean to be rude, sir, but what about your food?"

He smiles. "What's ours is yours. Food included."

I'm so happy, I want to hug Mikayla. But my savior has disappeared somewhere in the sea of brown and gray surrounding me.

One thing about blue or red or chartreuse fur—it sure makes it easier to find your friends.

A muscular gray mouse pops out from the crowd clustered behind the elderly James the Wise. "We'll show you around. Rustle you up some grub, too. I'm Gabriel. This is my sister Gwindell," he says, pointing to a smaller gray mouse.

I smile shyly. "Um, hi. Do either of you know where Mikayla went?"

"Away," says Gwindell with a wave of her paw.

"She's like that. Sort of artsy-fartsy, if you know what I mean."

"She's a wonderful singer," I say.

Gabriel laughs. "A singer?"

"Impossible," says Gwindell. "Girls don't sing. I should know."

"Come on, Isaiah," says Gabriel, clapping me on the back. "This way to the breakfast buffet. The Brophys had bacon this morning!"

"Bacon?" I say. "What's that?"

"A human word."

"But what does this word *bacon* mean?"

"'Crispy deliciousness,'" says Gwindell. "You'll see!"

CHAPTER 14

*"Burdens always seem lighter
when friends help you carry them."*
—Isaiah

After our feast of bacon and more bacon (which, by the way, *is* the most crisply delicious food I have ever nibbled), Gabriel and Gwindell give me a quick tour of their burrow.

Their home is extremely clean and well organized—another thing mice are particularly good at. It's true. Rats may be dirty, but we mice like to stay clean and dry at all times. It's why I took particular offense at that rolling-pin-hurling baker when she called me a filthy rodent. I take great pride in my cleanliness. In a way, we mice bathe so often, we're similar to cats.

Yipes!

I did it again. I just scared myself by saying *cat*. I have to stop doing that.

"This here is the sleeping area," says Gabriel, as we scurry past a tidy row of straw beds tucked into a cozy nook.

"You've already seen the dining area," adds Gwindell. "Please don't bring any food or beverages to bed with you."

"Unless you want ants," says Gabriel with a shudder of disgust.

"And way down here," says Gwindell, as we continue down a tunnel, "is the...you know..."

"Always do you-know-what down there," adds Gabriel.

Actually, I don't know, but it sure smells foul. Like my cedar shavings after I...

Oh.

"You do your droppings all the way down here?" I ask.

"Well, duh," says Gabriel. "You don't want to drop where you eat or sleep, do you?"

"No," I say, with another nervous chuckle. "Of course not. That would be unsanitary."

"And gross," adds Gwindell. "Seriously gross."

But guess what? That's exactly what they made us do back at the Horrible Place. It was one of the things that made it so spectacularly awful. Especially if you ever rolled over in your sleep. Not that I ever did. I was usually too afraid to even close my eyes.

"So," says Gabriel, "you ready to check out the rest of the house?"

"There's more?"

"Lots more. And—there might be more bacon."

"Or Doritos," adds Gwindell.

"Doritos," I say. "D-O-R-I-T-O-S."

"Huh?"

"Nothing."

Most mice can't spell. I, of course, can. I also can't forget that crumpled bag I saw before I reached the ledge outside the Horrible Place. Those were Doritos, too.

"What exactly are Doritos?" I ask.

"More Brophy deliciousness," says Gabriel.

"If you get the ones that taste like nacho cheese," says Gwindell, "and not the ones that smell like salad dressing or Buffalo wings."

I have no idea what she means, but there's no time to ask. We scamper, single file, through the walls and into the beams underneath a sagging floor. Gabriel leads the way. He's one of those mice who automatically makes everybody else feel safer, like my big brother Benji.

"With three of us," says Gabriel, "we should be able to bring back a huge haul!"

"This way," says Gwindell. "We'll take the sink drain. It'll put us right in the Brophys' kitchen."

We scuttle up the side of the pipe and into a cabinet cluttered with cans, spray bottles, and another overflowing trash can.

"Slightly used food!" I say, darting up the side of the garbage pail. "There's a half-eaten sandwich in here," I report. "Smells meaty, too! I see a slice of pizza with a chomp mark in it."

"Leave it," says Gabriel. "These Brophys are such pigs, we'll soon be eating high off the hog. No need to dip into their half-chewed garbage scraps."

"Come on," says Gwindell. "Hop down. We need your help shoving open this cabinet door. Mr. Brophy always leaves a heap of dirty work clothes lying on the other side. Stops it from swinging open."

I jump down, scoot around a bottle of something labeled "All Purpose Cleaner" that looks like it's never been used, and join Gwindell and Gabriel behind the kitchen cabinet door.

"Brace your feet," instructs Gabe. "Lean against the wood. One, two, three, push!"

We all shove. The door budges open just a crack.

"Dirty work clothes," says Gwindell, sniffing the air. "Again."

I sniff, too. The scent is vaguely familiar and reminds me—just for a second—of home.

Then the scent of hot food wafts in through the open cabinet door. We could push again. But, like I said, that first shove opened the cabinet just a crack.

And, as you might recall, a crack is all we mice ever need.

CHAPTER 15

"The apples on the other side of the wall always taste the sweetest. The Oreos, too."
—Isaiah

To call the Brophy home a pigsty would be an insult to pigs everywhere.

Crumpled food bags and rotting fruit are tossed higgledy-piggledy on the kitchen floor. There is also a large mountain of laundry piled in front of the kitchen sink. Crusty socks. Dirty underpants. And slimy green work clothes that look (and smell) strangely familiar.

I'm giving them a good sniff when Gabriel taps me on the shoulder.

"We came here to gather food, Isaiah, not to smell dirty laundry."

"Right. It's just that I think I've smelled something on these green pants and this green shirt before."

"Well, they've been heaped here for at least a week."

"But I didn't smell it here…"

"You guys?" cries Gwindell from up on the counter. "We've got cookies! Chocolate with chocolate chips!"

"Woohoo!" shouts Gabriel with a mighty tail pump. "Score."

He scoots up the side of the cabinetry. I scoot up after him.

"Food test!" declares Gwindell.

"Definitely," says Gabriel. "You see, Isaiah, before we drag a new, untested food item home to the burrow, we must make absolutely certain that it is safe for mousely consumption. Dig in!"

We do. And yummy mummy, they're delish!

"We should definitely drag a few of these back to the gang," says Gabriel.

Gwindell twitches her snout. "Mmmm. This box smells delicious, too!"

"No!" I shout. "Don't go in there."

"Why not? It smells so peanut buttery." She lunges for the brown box, and I dive to block her.

"It's a mousetrap!" I holler, reading what is written on the side of the cardboard mouse coffin. "The floor is covered with glue, and they've baited it with peanut butter. If you go in, you'll never come out!" Gwindell and her brother examine the box carefully.

"Why, those sneaky Brophys," says Gabriel. "How'd you figure out that it was a trap, Isaiah?"

"I, um, read the box."

"Huh?"

"Those are words," I say, pointing to the label. "Words tell you things."

Both Gabriel and Gwindell sort of stare at me.

"You're kind of different, aren't you?" says Gabriel.

"I suppose. Reading is just something I learned when I was young. It comes in quite handy. For instance, from reading, I know this box over here contains Fruity Pebbles."

"The Brophys eat rocks?" says Gwindell. "No wonder they all look so lumpy."

"And these are Double Stuf Oreos."

"Wow," says Gabriel. "They look doubly yummy."

"And," I say, "they're shaped like wheels so we can easily roll them back to the den!"

"Excellent idea!"

But just as we're about to trundle the first cookie wheel out of its crinkly plastic package, we hear footsteps. The heavy *clomp-flick-clomp* of a lazy walker wearing shoes with the laces untied.

"Hide!" whispers Gwindell.

The three of us scurry behind the cereal box. When we peer around the edge, I see a slovenly boy with a jiggly belly wearing a Chicago Bears football jersey, plaid shorts, and—yep—untied sneakers.

The boy is also wearing headphones that are blasting loud, ugly music. He finds a half-gallon jug of soda pop in the refrigerator and guzzles it straight out of the bottle. After he belches like a bullfrog, he starts making a sandwich, slapping ham, cheese, bologna, salami, more cheese, turkey, mayonnaise, ketchup, and corn chips on a bun.

"That's Dwayne," Gabriel whispers in my ear. "He's the Brophys' son. Their only child."

"That might be a good thing," I whisper back. "If he had any brothers or sisters, they'd probably starve."

"He's a first-class food fumbler," whispers Gwindell.

As if on cue, Dwayne grabs something out of the refrigerator, examines it for half a second, then tosses it uneaten over his shoulder.

"Oh, my," gasps Gwindell, smacking her lips. "That's a cream horn."

"What's a cream horn?" I ask. "An edible musical instrument?"

"No, my blue friend." Gabriel is practically drooling. "It's a tube of flaky pastry stuffed with fluffy white frosting. It's my favorite dessert in the world."

"Mine, too," adds Gwindell.

"Heck, everybody loves cream horns," says Gabriel. "Even artsy-fartsy Mikayla."

Well, that certainly ups my interest in Dwayne's

discarded dessert. "Why did the Brophy boy toss it on the floor?" I ask.

"He has so much food to choose from," says Gabriel, "he doesn't recognize the scrumptiousness he already holds in his hand. Whatever food he doesn't want, he just dumps on the floor for the cat to lick up."

I gulp. *"Cat?"*

"Oh, yes. The Brophys have a cat. A monster with evil yellow eyes."

"It's bald and has wrinkled, saggy skin," says Gwindell. "It's also a real killer."

I gulp again. "Is its name, by any chance, Lucifer?"

"Yes," says Gabriel. "How could you possibly know that?"

"We've met before." I tug nervously at my neck fur. "And I really hope it never happens again."

CHAPTER 16

"Fear and courage are brothers—
the kind that drive each other crazy."
—Isaiah

After building a sandwich thicker than a size-twelve work boot, Dwayne Brophy waddles out of the kitchen.

"He'll eat it on the sofa in the TV room," says Gabriel.

"It's what he does every day," adds Gwindell.

"But we need to hustle," says Gabriel. "Lucifer will soon be here to lick that cream horn clean. Cats love cream almost as much as they love munching mice."

I help Gabriel and Gwindell roll the cookies to the edge of the countertop.

"But how do we drop them down without cracking them into a thousand crumbs?" asks Gwindell, peering over the ledge.

I look around the countertop. "Easy," I say. "We give the cookies a cushion to land on."

I dash over to the stove and find a puffy, padded oven mitt. I clamp its hanger loop in my teeth and drag it back to the ledge.

"We'll shove this over first. It's spongy and fluffy. It'll be our target when we push the cookies over the precipice."

Gabriel and Gwindell look confused. "Huh?"

"*Precipice* is another word for the cliff created by the lip of the counter."

"Oh."

We slide the padded glove over the edge. It lands with a gentle *flop*. Next, we roll the cookies. They make a soft landing. No crumbling. No shattering. No squished double stuf in the Oreos.

"You are one clever mouse, Isaiah!" exclaims Gabriel. "But we'd better hurry. Lucifer is always on the prowl."

We zip down the sides of the cabinetry and roll the cookies under the sink. Next, hugging the baseboards, we head over to the front of the refrigerator, where Dwayne dropped all sorts of cheese and meat on the floor while making his sandwich.

"An excellent haul," says Gabriel when all the food is safely stashed behind the cabinet door. "Let's head for home and celebrate with a family feast!"

I hesitate.

I'm thinking about that cream horn sitting in the middle of the floor. And how, according to Gwindell, it is Mikayla's favorite dessert. Perhaps, if I present her with such a yummy-mummy treat, she'll sing for me again.

But Lucifer could appear at any moment. And, as you know, I'm not the bravest mouse in the burrow.

"Wait here, you two," I say, then take a deep breath.

For the first time in my life, I realize that courage is a strange mix of nerves and nuttiness. You have to be kind of crazy to go for a cream horn when you know an evil cat could attack you at any second.

But even though it is an incredibly dangerous (and, dare I say, *stupid?*) thing to do, I dash to the middle of the kitchen floor. Heart pounding, I curl the flaky pastry in my arms and scamper back to rejoin my two friends under the sink.

"You certainly are a brave little mouse," says Gabriel.

"Not really," I say. "I did it for a friend."

That night, we have a huge family dinner—over two hundred mice feasting on the meat and treats Gabriel, Gwindell, and I hauled home from the Brophys' kitchen. It feels like the holiday humans call Thanksgiving, especially when James the Wise rises from his thimble chair to give the blessing.

"For this bounty, dear Mouse God, we are indeed grateful. Thank you for leading us into the Land of the Brophys, where every mouse can eat his fill and still find plenty to share with his family. For that is the greatest blessing of them all: family."

Everyone at the table nods and repeats the refrain: "Family!"

I don't think there has ever been a finer feast. The meat, cheese, and cookies are delish, especially when sprinkled with bacon bits.

But the cream horn, sliced into thin pieces with a saw made out of dental floss, tastes as heavenly as Mikayla's voice.

She's sitting at the far end of the table, looking extremely happy as she licks the white frosting off her whiskers. In fact, she seems like she might burst into song at any moment.

She doesn't, of course. Girl mice aren't supposed to be able to sing.

When the table is cleared and the dishes put away, it's time to curl up with my new family for the night.

Family.

James the Wise was correct. It is such a warm and wonderful word. The coziest word of them all. If you ask me, family is the true cream horn of life, filled with sweetness. Worth risking your life for.

So I whisper another prayer of mouse gratitude.

I am thankful to be with Mikayla's family.

And I hope that I'll once again find my own.

CHAPTER 17

"It's very important to have something to do, something to love, and something to hope for."
—Isaiah

The next morning, I'm up before everyone else because, as you recall, most mice are nocturnal *and* crepuscular, which means they don't see much of the morning past dawn's first light.

I, however, was put on the human's schedule ever since I was born. So, while they all snooze, I'm alone with my thoughts.

My mind races with memories of my family. My secret wish? That they all might escape the Horrible Place and come live with me and my new friends under the Brophy house. There's plenty of room, and the Brophys leave enough food lying around for half a dozen mice families. We could easily feed six hundred with just one of Dwayne's belly-bomber sandwiches.

Hours later, at dusk, my adoptive brothers and sisters begin to stir.

I see Mikayla in the kitchen, cleaning up from last night's fantastic feast.

Her brown fur is so shiny and beautiful. I can tell she just brushed it—it glistens in the soft light leaking through the burrow's ceiling.

She, of course, doesn't notice me noticing her. That's okay. But I'd give anything for another burst of bravery—just enough courage to ask her to sing again. Not *for* me, just *near* me so I can hear it.

But ever since she brought me here and introduced me to her extended family, the loveliest mouse I have ever met has mostly ignored me. She's not being nasty or rude. Just indifferent.

I wonder if she even knows that I'm the one who brought home the cream horn last night. Or that I risked my life snatching it for her.

Probably not. And if she did, I'm afraid she wouldn't be impressed or even care.

And so I sigh.

I've been doing a lot of sighing ever since I first set eyes on my beautiful brown songstress.

While I'm standing there, sighing repeatedly and feeling sort of sad and sorry for myself, Gabriel and Gwindell come whipping around a corner with four other mice.

"Come on, Isaiah," says Gabriel. "Time for another food run!"

"It's dinnertime up at the Brophys'," explains

Gwindell. "That means it'll soon be raining food underneath their dining room table!"

"We have to be fast about it," adds Gabriel. "Dawdling at night is dangerous because Lucifer will be wide awake."

Yes, cats are nocturnal creatures, too. Mouse life would be so much easier if mice weren't on the same schedule as their primary predator.

So the seven of us scamper through the wall tunnels, up the sink pipe, and across the kitchen floor and into the Brophys' dining room.

It's not a pretty sight.

Mostly, what we see are butts. Big, chubby butts. They droop like saddlebags over the sides of creaky wooden chairs straining to hold that much weight.

"Pass the ketchup," says Mr. Brophy.

"You're putting ketchup on your mashed potatoes?" says a largish woman who I assume to be Mrs. Brophy.

"Yes," says Mr. Brophy. "We're all out of ding-dang mayonnaise. And I drank all the gravy."

"I like to jab a whole stick of butter into my mashed potatoes," says Dwayne as he scoops up a big mound of lumpy yellow goop. "Butter makes everything better!"

He moans with delight as he shoves the enormous ball of buttery mush into his mouth.

In fact, all the Brophys *nom-nom-nom* very loudly while they eat. Fireworks could explode in the kitchen and they probably wouldn't hear a pop.

Dwayne shovels another helping of buttery potatoes toward his mouth. Half of it tumbles like a doughy boulder from his lips to his chest to the floor.

"Go!" whispers Gabriel.

Gwindell tears across the floor lightning fast, picks up the ball of glop, and, without breaking stride, carries it off to the kitchen cabinet.

The next food to fall is a whole slice of meatloaf that Mrs. Brody fumbles when her husband asks for thirds.

Two mice dash out and catch the slab of meat before it even hits the rug.

Then Dwayne swipes his buttery face with a cloth napkin, which he tosses to the floor.

And that gives me a brilliant idea!

CHAPTER 18

"No team works without teamwork."
—Isaiah

I feel just like my big brother Benji, hatching a plan. I ask Gabriel and two other mice named Gilbert and George to help me turn Dwayne's napkin into a food net.

"We'll each grab a corner and stretch it out," I explain. "When the food falls, all we have to do is catch it in the napkin. We can carry a much heavier load that way than we ever could in our paws!"

"And when it's full," says Gabriel, picking up on my idea, "we can tie the four corners in a knot to make a sack."

The four of us hightail it under the table. The

Brophys are so busy stuffing their faces, they don't notice as we dart under their chairs and dash between their feet.

In no time at all, we catch a couple dinner rolls, another mound of mashed potatoes, an ear of corn, more mashed potatoes, a second slab of meat-loaf, and a whole helping of yummy-mummy broccoli that Dwayne scraped off his plate when his mother wasn't looking.

We drag our bulging feedbag across the floor while the Brophys move on to dessert, scarfing down dozens of jelly-filled doughnut holes. As a few tumble off the Brophys' bellies and drop to the floor, two mice named Geoffrey and Gilligan race to catch them.

Meanwhile, the other mice and I drag our hefty bag of food back to the kitchen. We're so happy, we sing a little as we go (mouse voices are ultrasonic, so the Brophys can't hear us). We don't sound nearly as good as Mikayla, of course, but music makes any chore much more enjoyable.

Our food sack is so huge, we have to unload it under the sink and carry the delicious goodies, one by one, down the drainpipe hole.

Now our singing echoes off the wooden walls of the crawl space. It sounds magnificent, like we're in a concert hall.

"I wish I could hear Mikayla sing in this echo chamber," I say to Gabriel. "I suspect it might give my goosebumps goosebumps!"

"Mikayla can't sing," says Gabriel with a chuckle. "We told you. She's a girl."

"Mikayla has an amazing singing voice. I've heard it. And, paws crossed, I hope to hear her sing again."

Gabriel shakes his head. "Girl mice don't sing. Singing's only for boys."

I just grin because I sense that I am the only mouse in the burrow who knows the truth about Mikayla and her hidden talent. Somehow, that makes me feel closer to her—no matter how distant she's been acting toward me.

"Where are those doughnuts?" asks Gabriel, once all the other foodstuffs are secure in the tunnel beneath the sink drain.

"Um, we dropped them," admit Geoffrey and Gilligan, both of whom appear to be even younger than me. "The jelly made them too slippery for us to carry all the way across the kitchen."

Gabriel shakes his head. "Gwindell will be so disappointed. She loves those jelly balls."

"Well," I say, remembering Mikayla's similar fondness for sweets, "it's really not a proper family feast without some kind of yummy-mummy dessert. Let's go back and grab them!"

So we all troop out from under the sink, whistling as we march across the floor like a merry mouse parade.

It's fun.

Until it isn't.

CHAPTER 19

**"The mouse that has but one hole
is soon caught."**
—Isaiah

Lucifer—the wrinkle-skinned cat with the evil yellow eyes—is prowling along the kitchen's cluttered countertops, looking for something to eat.

He spies the doughnut balls in the middle of the room.

And then he sees us.

He purrs. I think that means he prefers mouse-filled mice to jelly-filled doughnuts. I stand frozen in my tracks, halfway between the sink and the fallen goodies.

What to do? What to do?

Abandon dessert and flee? Or risk my life and go for the treats?

Once again, I ask myself that age-old question: Am I a man or a mouse?

Well, I'm definitely a mouse, and after spending some time observing the Brophys, I'm not sure I ever want to be a man. But I *do* want Mikayla to have fond memories of the time we spent in the burrow, even if we don't spend much of it together.

Therefore, ignoring all my cowardly fears and disregarding all my completely rational survival instincts, I race across the kitchen floor.

"Isaiah!" shrieks Gabriel, who's taken up a hiding place under the refrigerator. "What in the name of Mouse God are you doing?"

"Only what any music-loving mouse must do!" I screech wildly as I zig, zag, and zip across the floor.

Up on the counter, Lucifer is mesmerized by my swift, snakelike moves. Cats love to watch things whizz across the floor. Reflections. Laser pointers. *Mice.*

But after they're done being mesmerized, typically, they pounce. I don't have much time.

I skid to a stop at the doughnut balls and lob them backward over my head, one by one.

"Got it!" shouts Gilligan behind me.

"This one's for you, Geoffrey!" I shout. I spin around and kick another ball. It zooms through the air to Geoffrey, who comes running out of his hiding place to catch it on the fly.

"Tell everybody dessert's on me!" I shout.

The other mice flee, taking all the doughnut holes I could save.

Because Lucifer springs into action. He leaps off the counter, knocking over a roll of paper towels and a cake pan. His claws are out, and I'm certain he knows how to use them.

A split second before he shreds my tiny body into minced mouse meat, I dart sideways. Lucifer's claws end up scarring the wooden floor instead of my back.

Once again, my treadmill workouts come in handy. Legs pumping, I sprint for the baseboards. Lucifer screeches angrily and sprints after me.

Thinking fast, I ladder up the drawer pulls and scurry across the cluttered countertop. Lucifer jumps up behind me. I dodge around stacks of dirty dishes and hurdle over some filthy mugs. Lucifer barrels into a few and sends china crashing to the floor. He also takes out a pig-shaped cookie jar and a plastic pasta bin filled with fusilli that pitter-patters as it crashes to the floor.

While Lucifer slips and slides on the rolling noodles, I leap off the counter, scamper out of the kitchen, and race into what appears to be Dwayne Brophy's bedroom.

There are crumpled chip bags, empty soda pop bottles, and discarded Hot Pockets wrappers scattered everywhere. I scrunch up my nose and tunnel under a heap of Dwayne's dirty underpants.

The stench might kill me before the cat does.

CHAPTER 20

"He who fights and runs away
lives to eat dessert another day."
—Isaiah

As I wiggle farther into the heap of soiled laundry, Lucifer swats at the twitching bulges betraying my every move. It's almost as if he has X-ray vision as he bops at me through the rippling ocean of tossed T-shirts, socks, and underwear.

Desperate for a better hiding place, I scuttle across the floor and dive for one of Dwayne's shoes.

Not a great idea.

Lucifer slams into the shoe, knocking it—and me—sideways.

I'm seeing stars. My ears are ringing.

Lucifer is hissing happily. He's ready to play Cat

and Mouse with my life again. He rears back a paw to smack me, and I brace myself to be a furry tennis ball.

He bats me once, and I bounce off the TV stand. He bats me again, and I bang into a stinky sneaker. I can't take many more whacks to the head. Those stars I was seeing have turned into constellations.

And so I go with my last remaining trick.

"WOOF!" I bark at the top of my lungs. "WOOF-WOOF!"

I can do a pretty good vocal impression of this nasty guard dog I knew back at the Horrible Place.

Stunned, Lucifer freezes mid-swat.

My Doberman pinscher impersonation is good enough to make his eyes bug out of his head, Chihuahua-style. I seize my chance before Lucifer can seize me. The hairless hairball hacker has given me a small opening, and a small opening is all a mouse ever really needs.

I tear out of the bedroom and zoom back to the kitchen.

Beyond it, past the refrigerator, is a smaller room filled with muddy work boots and filthy plaid jackets. And, hidey-ho, I see another, extremely conveniently located pet door to the outside.

I take off like a rocket and fly through the rubber flap. Lucifer, who is right behind me, lunges for the pet door, too. But, judging by the very loud yowl I hear behind me, I'm pretty sure he missed.

CHAPTER 21

*"Be careful with your heart.
Once it's broken it's hard to find spare parts."*
—Isaiah

Fortunately, I quickly find the oily streak Mikayla and I first followed around the Brophy home. It leads me out of the weedy backyard and down into the cozy communal burrow.

"He's alive!" cries Gabriel when I make my entrance. "Isaiah survived!"

Everyone is gathered around the table, their acorn-shell bowls loaded down with dinner—and our hard-won doughnut holes.

James the Wise rises from his thimble throne.

"Well done, Isaiah! Gabriel and Gilbert told us how you bravely confronted the cunning sphynx cat, Lucifer. How you protected your brethren and

provided us with this evening's meal, one of the finest my tired old mouse eyes have ever seen. From this day forward, mice shall sing of your triumph over the evil-eyed destroyer."

He holds up a kernel of corn, freshly plucked from the cob we snagged under the table with Dwayne's soiled napkin. "I raise this bite to you, Isaiah the Brave. Hip! Hip!"

"Hidey-ho!" shout all my new brothers and sisters and second cousins once removed.

Isaiah the Brave?

Well, I don't know about that. "Isaiah the Foolish" might be a more appropriate title for a mouse willing to risk his life on the off chance that his crazy antics might inspire the fairest creature in all the land to once more sing her dulcet melodies.

Speaking of Mikayla, I see her seated at the far end of the table. I bustle over to her, earning another hearty round of "Hip, hip, hidey-hos" and high-fives along the way.

"Miss Mikayla, I hope you enjoy tonight's dessert as much as you seemed to enjoy the cream horn last night. As you may have heard from Gabriel or Gwindell, I risked my life fetching both treats especially for you."

I twirl a paw in front of my face and bow rather elegantly, if I do say so myself.

"Thank you, Isaiah," says Mikayla. "You are nearly as sweet as the sugar on this doughnut ball."

I'm blushing. That means my blue cheeks are turning purple.

Mikayla fixes me with a look. By the way, her big brown eyes not only match her fur, but also are extremely dreamy.

"Isaiah," she says, her voice sweet and mellow, "I know how much you say you enjoyed what you heard when we first met."

This is it! Mikayla's about to express her eternal gratitude for my dessert-scavenging heroics by singing to me again.

She takes a deep breath. Here it comes!

"But I don't sing," she whispers.

Disappointed, I say, "Yes, you do. I heard you."

"Only because I didn't know you were there." She's still whispering. Making sure no one else can hear what she's telling me. "Girls don't sing."

"B-b-but..."

She heaves a frustrated sigh. "You're not a normal mouse, so you don't understand. In this family, girls aren't supposed to sing. We're supposed to wash and dry acorn cups and take care of the babies. I might not like it, but that's just the way it is. Being different isn't a good thing."

And then she turns to the young mouse seated beside her. An infant who needs help slicing her meatloaf.

That's when it hits me.

Mikayla is telling me that no matter how much I try, no matter how many desserts I heroically haul into the den, this burrow will never be my true home. Mikayla's mischief will never be my true family.

I'm just too ridiculously different.

I quietly slip out of the dining hall. I'm going to skip dinner. All I want to do is lie down in a bed of dry straw where I can sigh and stare at the ceiling.

Realizing the sad truth about my even sadder situation leaves me feeling even bluer than my very blue fur.

CHAPTER 22

"A mouse's best teacher
is his last mistake."
—Isaiah

Bright and early the next morning, while Mikayla and the rest of her nocturnal mouse mischief snooze, I go outside for some fresh air.

Yes, this is further proof of just how different we are.

I'm outside in the dewy lawn, feeling the sunshine warm my whiskers. Mikayla and her family remain snug in their beds, dreaming of meatloaf and mashed potatoes falling from the sky.

I have decided, after much soul-searching, that I need to refocus my efforts. I will no longer be chiefly concerned with scavenging for tasty treats in the hope that they might, somehow, inspire Mikayla to sing for me. Instead, I will use my unusual skills and talents in a renewed attempt to reunite with my real family—the mischief where all the mice are just as peculiar as me. Some even have vastly superior vocabularies and say things like "vastly superior" all the time.

Fearing that the morning dew might have washed away my trail here in Suburbia, I go for a stroll to re-mark the territory with my distinctive scent, my "Eau de Isaiah," if you will. If Winnie or Abe pick up one whiff of my fragrant aroma, I feel quite certain they'll come running to find me.

As I scurry around the neighborhood, rubbing up against anything and everything that's rubbable, I notice how much nicer all the other homes on this street are compared to the Brophys' dilapidated dwelling. For instance, the house across the street from the Brophys' is very tidy and neat, with lots of flowers and bright green grass.

As I'm admiring the view, a shadow flits in a swooping arc across the glistening emerald lawn. And then it swoops past again.

I look up. *Yipes!*

It's a bird. Circling directly overhead.

As you know, I am not a big fan of birds. However, birds are HUGE fans of mice.

They like to eat us.

This undoubtedly hungry bird has me in its sights. I sense it will soon swoop in for the kill.

But then there's a noise. A metallic clank and thud. Startled, the bird flaps its wings and flies away.

I look over to the front porch. A young girl in a bathrobe just yanked open a heavy wooden door so hard, she sent its brass knocker banging against it.

The girl picks up a newspaper wrapped in bright blue plastic and heads back inside.

Fearful that the hungry bird might soon return, I run around to the back of the house where the treetops are leafy—thick enough to block a bird's-eye view of my movements.

Well, hidey-ho and what do you know? This house has a pet door, too.

During my short time in Suburbia, I've noticed that humans, much like mice, tend to do things in groups. They drive the same kind of cars. They install pet doors. They decorate their grounds with the same types of flowers, shrubberies, and lawn ornaments. Many even have bird feeders and birdbaths in their backyards.

This one does.

And both are fully occupied by birds tough enough to scare off the squirrels.

An angry blue jay nibbling a beak-load of seeds flicks his head in my direction.

I can read his mind just by studying his beady little eyes and watching his wings twitch: *Hmmm,* he seems to be thinking. *A juicy mouse or dry sunflower seeds? Which would be the more delicious choice?*

I know he'll go for me instead of the measly seeds. Because birds always choose mice over rice.

So I make my own choice. I go for the pet door at the back of the house.

And, just like that, I am once again in a whole new world.

CHAPTER 23

"If you don't want trouble,
don't go looking for it."
—Isaiah

O n the other side of the pet door, there is a dog.
I should've seen that coming.

Who needs a pet door without a pet?

This time, it's a very small dog. With a pink bow and a pink collar.

Since the dog appears to be friendly (her tail is wagging) and somewhat cute, I attempt communicating with her via mental telepathy.

"Hello, friendly dog. My name is Isaiah."

The dog cocks her head, as if she understands what I am thinking. So I keep going.

"I come in peace and hope that you and I may soon become fast friends, for we share a mutual enemy: cats. Especially the hairless variety. Might I kindly enter your kitchen, as I am on a quest for breakfast? Just for myself, mind you. My days of being a *mus* and scavenging for others are officially over. I'd also like to add that you have excellent taste in accessories. That pink bow looks very nice on you."

The dog pants. Wags her tail.

And cries, "YIP!"

Very loudly. As you might recall, my ears are quite sensitive, especially to yips and/or yaps.

"YIP! YAP! YIP!"

Perhaps the dog is simply attempting to say hello in its somewhat primitive canine language. So, I return the greeting.

"YIP!" I shout.

"YIPES!" squeaks the dog.

Oh, dear. I think I scared her. Claws clicking, she scampers away, her tail drooping between her hind legs.

Fascinating. I actually scared off a creature much larger than myself. I am starting to understand why

Benji and so many other members of my real family kept encouraging me to be more courageous. Being brave has its rewards.

For instance, now that the "guard dog" has abandoned her post, I notice that the neat and tidy countertops of this kitchen hold a cornucopia of tasty delights. I see fruit in a bowl. Bread on a cutting board. And, judging by the sugary-cinnamon smell, something yummy-mummy in a cardboard box.

Should I go for the healthier, more nutritious fruit, or the mysterious sweet treat in the box?

Easiest decision ever!

I climb up the back of a rolling chair and jump off it to a computer desk, which I use as a springboard to take me up to the countertop and the sweet-smelling blue box.

The box has a plastic window through which I can see a rugged landscape of sweet brown-sugar lumps. I read the words printed around the plastic window: "Entenmann's Ultimate Crumb Cake."

Well, hidey-ho.

This is no ordinary crumb cake. This is the *ultimate*. The high point of crumb cake creation. The very peak of crumb-cakiness.

I must sample it immediately.

The thin plastic window is easy to slice through with a flick of my claws. In no time, I am inside the box, rolling around in the clumps of buttery, cinnamony brown sugar. I bury my face in the cake.

It's delicious. Dare I say, the ultimate?

I come up for air, ready to dive in for more moist and spongy cake. That's when the girl comes into the kitchen.

Remember her? The one in the bathrobe on the front porch? She's carrying a rolled-up newspaper.

And now I'm noticing something else. Not to be rude, but she's a little odd-looking. Even though she appears to be a human teenager, her hair is frosty white—even her eyelashes. And her eyes? Why, they're bluer than my fur.

I also think she might be ill. She has a thermometer dangling out of her mouth. That means she could be running a fever.

Oh, I hope she isn't contagious. Humans are so worried about mice and the diseases we supposedly carry (confusing us, once again, with rats!), but let's be honest here—humans carry many more diseases than mice.

Oh, no. She just spotted me. Her mouth flies open.

There goes the thermometer. It tumbles out of her lips and crashes on the floor. I have to remember to watch out for those glass shards when she chases me across the kitchen.

And then, of course, she does something that, as a mouse, I'm very used to seeing and hearing.

She screams.

"EEEEEEK!"

CHAPTER 24

"Never dance on the nose
of a sleeping cat."
—Isaiah

I need for Little Miss Shrieksalot to *calm down immediately!*

Otherwise, some adult humans might come running into this kitchen and whack me with a rolled-up newspaper.

Wait a second. *She* has a rolled-up newspaper! And she's coming right for me, ready to smash me into the cake! Trapped by the plastic window, there's no escape.

I have no choice. I have to stop her.

"STOP!" I shout.

Okay. That didn't work. I forgot that mouse voices are ultrasonic, at a superhigh frequency that humans can't hear.

Her crystal-blue eyes have just about popped out of her skull, and now she's screaming even louder. The pitch of her shriek is three octaves higher, too, almost reaching mouse levels. In fact, it's so high, I have to cover my ears and duck down in the cake box. Maybe if I bury my head in the crumbs on top...

"That's my breakfast!" the girl screeches. "You've contaminated my crumb cake. Crumb cake is my favorite! *Agghhhhh!*"

O-kay. This white-haired banshee is definitely freaking me out. While she's busy screaming at me, I move to the hole I made in the plastic.

She lifts that rolled-up newspaper and rears it back like it's a hatchet.

That gives me a fraction of a second to do something that I know is absolutely, strictly forbidden. I've never done it in front of a human because it would've made life inside the Horrible Place even more horrible. It's definitely dangerous and probably dumb.

But the girl is lining up her shot. I need to do it now.

I explode out of the box. Sprint across the counter. Jump down to the desk.

And I dance.

On the computer keyboard.

This makes the girl even more furious.

She lowers her weapon, but she's still yelling at me. "Get off the keyboard, mouse! If you break it, I'll break *you!*"

As I dance across the clacking keys, I'm doing everything I can to get the girl to look up at the computer screen. Waving my arms. Cocking my head. Pointing with my tail.

She must think it's all part of the choreography.

"LOOK!" I squeak desperately.

She just narrows her eyes and raises that rolled-up newspaper again. "I warned you, mouse."

"PLEASE!" I cry, but of course, the girl can't hear me.

I need her to look at the computer screen before she clubs me across the kitchen like I'm a fuzzy blue golf ball.

I dance faster. I furiously flap my arms, my head, and my tail toward the screen.

She's coming at me. Fast.

She raises the newspaper high above her head.

I close my eyes. I know what's coming. I brace for it.

And then—

CHAPTER 25

**"Sometimes, words are worth
a thousand words."
—Isaiah**

I peel open one eye.

Terrified, but squinting, I can see that the girl is still holding the rolled-up newspaper over her right shoulder.

But her eyes are fixed on the computer screen.

"What the…" she mumbles.

She leans in to read what is written in strings of glowing letters.

She finally lowers her weapon.

"'Chill please?'" she reads aloud.

Now she's staring at me. Quizzically. I believe the young girl has just realized that I am not your

chill please? chill please?
chill please? chill please?
chill please? chill please?
chill please? chill please?
chill please?

ordinary, run-of-the-mill house mouse. She knows that I am definitely different. Well, I *am* blue. She's probably noticed that by now, too.

She leans in to study me more closely. I don't mind. I like her curious look much more than the murderous glare she had a few seconds ago. This is progress. I let out a sigh of relief. Fluff up my fur. Pat it down. When I panic, it gets a little cowlicky.

"Did you type those words?" she asks me.

I've never had a human wait for an answer from me before. I nod.

"Are *chill* and *please* the only two words you know how to type? Did somebody teach you to do that at, like, a mouse circus or something?"

That makes me grin.

I tap-dance across the keyboard in a quick six-step skip and hop: "h-a-r-d-l-y."

"Hardly what? Which question are you answering? The one about the mouse circus or how many words you know?"

Ah-ha. She makes a good point.

And so, in reply, I traipse across the keys like the Mouse King in the *Nutcracker* ballet, which I saw once on TV at the Horrible Place.

Here is what I type:

"forgive me. i did not mean to confuse you with my seemingly vague response to your query. no, i have never been in a mouse circus. and yes, i do have a very large, dare i say voluminous, vocabulary. at the time, however, i sensed that brevity and clarity were of paramount importance. 'chill' and 'please' communicated, in my humble opinion, my immediate desire with a great deal of efficiency and urgency, wouldn't you agree?"

The girl shakes her head and laughs. "Totally," she says.

I'm laughing now, too, in sheer relief.

I type out my own quick idea: "how about an ice-breaker?"

"Definitely, icebreaker. I'm Hailey. Who are you?"

I type it out for her.

isaiah

CHAPTER 26

*"Be friends with good people and
you will increase their number."*
—Isaiah

Hailey is actually very nice—especially when she's not about to swat me with a rolled-up newspaper-weapon.

"How'd you do that?" she asks. "How'd you type all those words?"

I type my answer: "rather well, wouldn't you agree?"

She laughs. "Yep. You're pretty amazing. Especially for a mouse."

"thank you, hailey. actually, many mice are amazing, but we are seldom given the chance to demonstrate our unique talents in front of humans. also, i apologize for not capitalizing letters that should be capitalized, like that 'i' back there and for not always using proper punctuation. it is hard for me to put one foot on the shift key and another on the letter i wish to type. especially when i am typing a y or h or something in the middle of the keyboard. i would need to do a split and rip my pants if i wore pants which i don't because, as you have already noticed, i am a mouse."

"You're also blue," says Hailey. "And what's up with that tag on your ear?"

I really don't want to get into my past and the things that were done to me and my family back at the Horrible Place, so I just shrug and type-dance: "i don't know. i have just always been blue, and i got this tag when i was born. by the way, in regards to capitalization, i know i could stomp on the caps lock key but THEN IT WOULD LOOK LIKE I WAS SHOUTING AT YOU."

Another laugh. "I'm glad I didn't go to school today. You're way more interesting than social studies or even math."

"do you like math?" I type.

It's Hailey's turn to shrug. "I don't like much of anything at school this year. We just moved to this 'burb. I'm the new kid in town so, you know, I don't have all that many friends. In fact, I have zip. Zero. Nada. The kids at school think I'm weird."

"why?" I ask.

She points at her white hair and her icy-blue eyes. "The way I look, I guess."

I type, "how old are you?"

"Twelve."

"well, no wonder your hair is so white. you are ancient. most mice only live one or two years. i, myself, hope to someday be twelve like you. then my fur might turn white like yours and i won't be so different from all the other mice. there are many white mice in the world, just not in my family."

"Hey, it's never easy being different."

"true. unless everybody around you is also different. for instance, my brother abe is red and very funny. my sister delphinia is purple and extremely strong. zoraster, he's pink, can always find the shortest route to the cheese no matter how deeply it's hidden in the maze."

While we're merrily chatting away, the little yappy dog I met behind the pet door proudly prances into the kitchen on clicking claws. And of course it yaps.

"No bark, Dolce," says Hailey. "No bark."

Dolce, of course, barks.

"She's actually very friendly," Hailey says to me. Dolce sits down and wags her tail. When she pants, her little pink tongue makes her look like a stuffed doggy toy.

"we've met," I reply. "and i would concur with your assessment. dolce is very sweet."

That makes Hailey smile because she knows that *dolce* means *sweet* in Italian.

Then she drops the bombshell that almost makes me wish I'd never stepped foot in this house. "We have a cat, too."

CHAPTER 27

"The cure for fifty enemies is one friend."
—Isaiah

My legs start trembling so much, this is what I type: "xcxcxcxcxcxc."

Hailey knows what I'm trying to say. "You don't need to worry, Isaiah. Red Boy is sweet, too."

A cat with fur nearly as red as Abe's slinks into the kitchen. He finds a spot of sunshine, stretches out his long body like he's made out of taffy, and slumps to the floor to nap in the warm pool of light.

Meanwhile, I remain *frozen* in fear.

"Um, would you like some double chocolate chip ice cream?" asks Hailey.

I'm able to budge my shoulders into a small shrug. I have no idea what she's talking about.

"Wait right there."

Don't worry, I want to type, as I keep one eye fixed on Red Boy, *I'm not moving a muscle!* But to type that message, I'd have to move lots of muscles. And as I mentioned earlier, cats *love* moving objects, especially mice. So I just stand perched on that key of C.

Hailey goes over to the refrigerator and returns with a scooper loaded with a melting mound of chocolate-chunk-studded creaminess. I lap it up the second she lowers it close enough to my snout. It's very cold but spectacular!

Red Boy sleeps through the whole thing. Even after Dolce started yapping again. I think the dog wanted some of the ice cream, too.

"Chocolate's not good for dogs," Hailey tells me. "I'm not sure about mice."

I shoot her a thumbs-up as I lick the bottom of the scoop bowl. I'm fine. All the mice at the Horrible Place can eat just about anything, even though all they ever fed us was kibble and sugar water.

Hailey finds a dog biscuit for Dolce, and I take that as my cue to leave.

"i must head home," I tap out as quietly as I can, hoping to let sleeping cats lie, as they say.

"I hope you'll visit again," says Hailey. She offers me her hand. "Friends?"

I nod and shake her pinky finger. We can be friends. For now, anyway.

You see, I have trouble completely trusting humans, even ones that seem as nice as Hailey.

Believe me, I have my reasons. Lots and lots of them.

CHAPTER 28

"A bird in the hand is better than a mouse in the mouth."
—Isaiah

I don't mean to whine, but life in Suburbia is fast becoming downright irritating.

I'm attempting to scamper home to the Brophys' ramshackle abode from my new friend Hailey's house when I see something on the lawn in front of me that makes me tremble in fear.

The shadow of a wingspan.

Another bird is directly overhead, sizing me up for dinner. It's a red-tailed hawk, to be precise. I recognize it from the fringe of fingertip-like feathers at the edges of its silhouette. We mice are big on memorizing the telltale shape of bird shadows.

And a red-tailed hawk is one we fear more than any other. They eat rats. Squirrels. Rabbits. They even eat other birds. We mice are mere appetizers.

I run faster.

The hawk's shadow looms larger. Only now, it's tucked its wings closer to its body because, oh no, it's dive-bombing me!

It's zooming straight at me!

I believe I would be out-of-my-mind petrified right now, but unfortunately, I don't have the time. *Dear Mouse God, please help!*

It's close, and coming closer.

With a painful clamp, the hawk snags me in its beak.

I close my eyes.

Goodbye, beautiful world.

I really would've liked to see my family just one more time. Perhaps, if I am very lucky, the angels in mouse heaven will sing as sweetly as Mikayla and there won't be any killer cats or yappy dogs or red-tailed hawks, either.

As I'm waiting for the snap of the beak—the chomp and the crunch that will signify the end of my life—I feel a weird, weightless sensation.

I also feel the grass disappear from under my feet. The hawk isn't gobbling me down in two swift gulps because...

Surprise! It's carrying me skyward!

I pry open one terrified eye.

I'm flying!

Flying is magnificent, something I've only ever done in my dreams. But since they were *my* dreams, there wasn't a mouse-munching bird of prey along for the ride, as there is in this nightmare.

Suddenly, we are climbing higher and higher, faster and faster. Oh, no. My whiskers are flapping in the

breeze. My blue fur is ruffling furiously. For once, I'm glad I probably taste so good that the hawk won't drop me, because it's a long way down to the ground.

Then the hawk angles its wings. Now we're plummeting even faster than we climbed.

Down, down, down...we're swooping into the branches of a leafy oak tree. The leaves slap and flap at us as we plunge through their green darkness.

And then the hawk opens its jaws.

I drop like a rock without a parachute.

For a second, I wonder if the hawk is playing with me like that evil cat Lucifer did, dropping then catching me like a toy. But no, the hawk is sailing away, leaving me to plummet all by myself. My descent becomes extremely rapid. I'm the one dive-bombing now—straight for a bumpy crook of a tree branch.

And knowing what I do about physics, hitting that hard branch will shatter every single bone in my tiny mouse body!

CHAPTER 29

**"If it's not one thing,
it's somebody's mother."
—Isaiah**

It's a miracle.

I don't die. My body doesn't slam into the rock-hard branch.

I make a soft landing.

Instead of hitting the gnarly tree limbs, I land in a nicely woven basket of twigs and straw and fluffy stuff.

Well played, I want to say to the hawk, feeling giddy with relief and happiness. *A perfect shot! Goooooaaaal!*

But then I hear a frenzied chorus of chirping.

Uh-oh.

I turn around. I'm surrounded by fuzzy chicks with their mouths wide open. This close up, they look like hungry dinosaurs made out of snow. I realize far too late why the marauding hawk just dropped me here.

I'm in its nest, and I am to be supper for its fuzzy-headed, big-eyed babies.

How very maternal of the hawk, to go out and fetch supper for its chicks. Her instinct to nurture newborn life is very touching.

Unless, of course, you happen to be *the supper!*

One of the cute little hawk chicks actually *lunges* at me. His instincts are kicking in, too: baby see mouse, baby *eat* mouse.

I dodge his beak. He snaps nothing but air as I scoot to the edge of the nest. Now two of the other chicks shuffle forward and bob their pointy beaks at me.

I shout one of the first human words I ever mastered. "STOP!"

Oops, I think I scared them. All of the chicks start chirping and crying. I have to cover my ears; their screeches and squawks are more piercing than anything I've ever heard inside a mouse nursery, even right before naptime.

While the baby birds are busy shrieking about the mean, yelling mouse their mommy dropped into their playpen, I seize my moment. I hop out of the nest and sink my claws into the bark of a nearby branch.

Oak bark is good for scampering. Lots of traction.

I scoot along that branch, jump to another, and continue laddering my way down from the tree. Moving quickly (I always seem to run faster when I know I'm running for my life), I reach the ground in twenty very rapid heartbeats.

I can see the Brophy house—it's such a mess, it's hard to miss. There's a pickup truck parked in the driveway. It has some kind of low roof on its back like a turtle shell.

I suppose this means Mr. Brophy is home and that the family will soon be dropping mass quantities of incredible edibles under the dining room table again. I scurry across the street.

Did I mention how downright irritating life in Suburbia is quickly becoming?

Because guess what's racing across the roadway with me? That's right. The same winged shadow. Mommy hawk is after me again.

No do-overs! I want to scream. But I don't. I'm too busy hightailing it to safety.

Fortunately, the Brophys aren't big on mowing their lawn. The swaying grass has grown nearly as high as their porch. It's like their own private wheat field.

The circling red-tailed hawk, even with its excellent vision, loses sight of me as I slowly crawl along on my belly. There is also a nice breeze blowing that makes the whole field of weeds sway like waves on the ocean. My movements aren't giving away my position. Mommy hawk abandons her quest. I see her soar off, searching for fresh prey.

Maybe I will live to see another day.

Then again, maybe not.

When you're a mouse, your chances for survival on any given day are always a little iffy.

CHAPTER 30

"Fools rush in
where mice fear to tread."
—**Isaiah**

I crawl into the burrow, just in time for the nightly food run.

Am I ready to face danger once again?

Absolutely not.

Am I ready to face Lucifer again?

Definitely no.

But when Gabriel asks, "Who's ready for a food run?" I raise my hand and volunteer. Perhaps because I spy someone new in tonight's scavenging party.

Mikayla.

As much as I was hurt when she told me how

different I am, I can't help admiring her. She is looking fetchingly fierce carrying a green plastic sword. I saw some just like it when the Long Coats had their holiday party last winter at the Horrible Place. Those colorful plastic swords had triumphantly skewered orange cheese cubes.

I pick my own scavenging tool, a cardboard stick with cotton swabs at each end (I guess to clean any food that's been on the floor beyond the five-second rule).

"I'm surprised and delighted to see you with the hunting party," I say to Mikayla as we make our way to the under-the-sink cabinet.

"In this family," she says, "we rotate tasks. We all take turns doing all the jobs. Tonight's your turn to do the dishes."

"Aha," I say, wiggling my whiskers the way my brother Rudolpho would. "I thought you told me only girls wash dishes, not that I'd mind. Next thing you know, you'll be saying that you're going to sing me a song. Just tell me when!"

"Probably never. Would never work for you?"

"Actually, I'd much prefer—"

Gabriel puts a paw to his lips to shush me. "Quiet, Isaiah. We don't want Lucifer to hear us coming."

"Right you are," I whisper. "Kindly forgive my unwise attempt at—"

"SHHHHH!"

The six of us press our shoulders against the cabinet door. Once again, it is rather hard to budge on account of all the clothes heaped on the other side. We slide, one by one, out of the gap and hide in the shadows under the cabinets.

Suddenly, we hear a jingle. But it isn't bells or

Lucifer's tags. It's something metallic, clinking and tinkling in the distance.

I have heard this sound before.

"Human!" whispers Gwindell. We all dive for hiding places in the mound of rumpled green work clothes. Once again, I wonder about the familiar scent, but not for long. The jingling draws near. I peek out of the shirt pocket I wiggled into and see the source of the sound. It's a key ring attached to the belt straining its way around Mr. Brophy's waist.

Of course! I should've figured this out sooner. This is why the pile of green work clothes smells so familiar. I've seen that ring of keys before.

Those are the keys that lock all the doors that keep my family imprisoned.

I look higher and take a good look at Mr. Brophy's face. He's the Mop Man at the Horrible Place!

CHAPTER 31

*"When you're riding a tiger,
it's hard to dismount."*
—Isaiah

"Luanne?" Mr. Brophy hollers. "Where are my ding-dang Doritos?"

"In the cabinet over the microwave."

"These are nacho cheese."

"Hands off!" shouts Dwayne from the dining room. "Those are mine."

"I know," says Mr. Brophy. "Where are my jalapeños?"

"They're already on the table," says Mrs. Brophy. "Behind the chicken bucket."

Mr. Brophy trudges out of the room. "Well, why

didn't you say so? Now I've wasted all that energy walking to the kitchen..."

The second he's gone, I turn to Gabriel. "We need to leave this place. Immediately!"

Gabriel sniffs the air. "But I smell grease. Fast food."

"Fast food is the best!" says Gilligan eagerly. "Fried chicken, fried onion rings, fried nuggets, French fries..."

"You don't understand. Mr. Brophy is a bad, bad man..."

Gabriel twitches his whiskers and smiles. "Maybe. But he brings home good, good food."

"Come on," says Mikayla. "Let's go see if they have fried apple pie!"

She leads the way up the cabinet pulls to the white paper bags blotted with oil splotches on their bottoms.

"There's another bag over there!" cries Gwindell. "Down on the floor by the cold box!"

She means the refrigerator.

Gwindell scampers off to examine the toppled white goody bag.

"Isn't this exciting?" Mikayla says to me.

And since she's actually talking to me, I pretend I'm having the time of my life. I act as if I don't know that Mr. Brophy is the evil Mop Man.

"Very exciting," I say. "A real thrill. However, I've never eaten fast food before."

"Oh, it's yummy," says Mikayla. "Especially the fried apple pies."

She offers me a steamy chunk. "Try it."

My weakness for apple pie takes over. "Maybe a quick nibble…"

I'm about to sink my teeth into the heavenly scented glop when I hear the most horrible sound in the mouse universe.

SNAP!

We freeze. All of our faces turn into masks of horror.

That sound is a mouse's *worst nightmare*.

CHAPTER 32

*"Don't go looking for danger.
It knows how to find you."*
—Isaiah

We race down from the cabinets and over to where Gwindell is lying on her side, writhing in pain.

"It's the jaws of death," gasps Mikayla.

"It was behind me," Gwindell moans. "I didn't see it."

"Take it easy," says Gabriel. "Try to calm down."

"Take it easy? Calm down? I'm trapped, Gabriel!"

It's true. Gwindell's tail and right rear leg are locked beneath the wicked hammer bar of a Victor Metal Pedal Mouse Trap.

There's a reason no mouse in history has ever named their child Victor.

"I'm too young to die!" whimpers Gwindell.

"You're not going to die," says Gabriel, his voice nearly as shaky as his sister's.

For centuries, we mice have known the danger lurking in mousetraps. We're taught about these evil contraptions from the day we're born. Nursery rhymes, such as "Mouse be nimble, mouse don't nap, mouse stay away from the mean mousetrap," are meant to teach us how to avoid these deviously simple killing devices.

But then a mouse will see a chunk of cheese sitting right there in the open. Overcome with cravings, she will believe with all her heart that she can sweep in and snatch the bait before the trap snaps shut.

Such wasn't the case for Gwindell. I suspect she attempted to tail-whip the cheese off the catch, but the trap was too fast. Now she has a broken leg and a severely pinched tail.

"We need to pry up the bar," I say.

"We can't," mutters Gabriel. "It's impossible."

"I am going to die!" shudders Gwindell.

"Come on," I say. "Lend a paw, everybody."

"It's hopeless," says Mikayla.

"Nothing's hopeless if we don't give up hope!" I grab hold of the bar. Try to raise it.

It won't budge.

Finally, the others join me. The five of us strain against the trap and try with all our might to lift it just high enough for Gwindell to roll free.

When my muscles feel like they might explode, Gabriel lets go.

"It's no use," he says.

The other mice follow his lead. I'm the last to loosen my grip.

"My tail is going numb," sobs Gwindell.

I'm about to make a suggestion, when Mr. Brophy comes stomping back into the kitchen.

"This way," I whisper.

We quickly slide Gwindell and her trap behind the refrigerator so we're all out of sight.

Mr. Brophy yanks open the refrigerator door. "They're still giving me grief about the one that got away," he hollers to his family in the dining room. "The blue one."

"Why do they need the blue one so bad?" screams his wife.

"Because he's the only one who got away." I hear glass jars jingling. "Where's the ding-dang root beer?"

"Behind the pickle tub," shouts Dwayne.

The kitchen floor creaks as Mr. Brophy marches back to the dining room.

Typically, this is when I would freak out. Panic.

Mr. Brophy just announced that the Long Coats at the Horrible Place are still searching for me. I wouldn't be surprised if my bright blue face was on some sort of wanted poster.

But even though Mr. Brophy could spot me at any moment and take me back to the Horrible Place, I refuse to abandon Gwindell. As they say in her family, "We leave no mouse behind!"

"We need to take Gwindell's body home," whispers Gabriel. "For her funeral."

Gwindell whimpers. "I can hear you."

"There's not going to be a funeral," I tell her. "There's going to be a homecoming party! We're going to save you, Gwindell. I give you my word."

She nods tearfully and manages a smile. She knows, as everyone does, that the word of a mouse is as solid as stone, and that I'll do anything I can to keep it.

Or die trying.

CHAPTER 33

*"A mouse of words and not of deeds
is like a garden full of weeds."*
—**Isaiah**

"It's impossible, Isaiah," says Gilligan.

"No mouse has ever outfoxed a trap like that," adds Gordon.

"We have to try," I say.

"Why?" asks Gabriel. "It'll only prolong Gwindell's suffering."

"I gave my word. And I have an idea…"

"I have an idea, too," says Gilligan. "Big Mr. Brophy is going to come back and trap us all!"

"Either that or step on us!" says Gordon, whose knees are knocking together.

"I just need a spoon." I gesture toward the counter near the sink. "There's probably one in that drawer up there. But to retrieve it, I'm going to need some assistance."

"There's probably another mousetrap in that drawer," whines Gordon. "That's probably where the Brophys hide their mousetraps!"

"Fine," I say. "I'll do it myself."

"No you won't," says Mikayla. "I'm coming with you."

"Me, too," says Gabriel.

The three of us scurry up the side of the cabinetry while Gilligan and Gordon go over to comfort Gwindell.

"What kind of flowers do you want at your funeral?" I hear Gordon ask her. "Dandelions or clover?"

Gwindell, of course, starts sobbing.

"We have to hurry," I tell Gabriel and Mikayla. "Those two are going to scare Gwindell to death."

We dash across the countertop to the edge overhanging a slender drawer.

"Hold on to my feet," I say. "I'm going over the ledge."

"Why?" asks Mikayla.

"I need to open that drawer down there. Hopefully, that's where the Brophys keep their cutlery. We can use one of the utensils to make a lever and pry Gwindell free."

"What's a lever?" asks Gabriel.

"One of the six simple machines. A lever is a stiff bar that rests on a support called a fulcrum. It'll help us lift a load that's too heavy to lift on our own."

Yes, it is amazing how much you can learn from books.

"Now, come on. We're running out of time. Grab hold of my ankles."

I seriously can't believe I'm about to do what I'm about to do. I crawl over the edge of the counter and dangle upside down like a trapeze artist.

I clamp down tight on the drawer handle. Now I have to use all my muscles, including the ones in my stomach, to tug on the handle. To wrench it forward.

At first it won't budge, but then Gabriel and Mikayla help out. When I tug, they yank back on my ankles to give me more oomph.

Soon, Gabriel is leading us in a chant. "Heave! Ho!"

On the "ho!" I tug and they yank. We start building up some momentum.

Slowly but steadily, the drawer slides open.

"Heave! Ho!"

That last pull is a doozy. The drawer is now open a good two inches.

I look into the drawer. Eureka! It is, indeed, filled with knives, forks, and spoons.

"I think a soup spoon will do the job nicely," I say. "Let go of my feet."

I drop face-first into the open drawer. The silverware clinks and clatters when I land.

"Are you okay?" asks Mikayla.

"Fine," I mumble, my nose stuck between the tines of a fork.

We hear Gilligan asking Gwindell if he can have

her bedding when she's dead. She wails loudly in response.

"Hurry," urges Gabriel. "Please."

I grab a spoon and try to raise it up over the side of the cabinet, but I can't do it. It's too heavy.

"You guys?" I say. "I need more help."

Mikayla and Gabriel look at each other. Shrug.

Inspired by my lunacy, they step off the edge of the kitchen counter and drop into my drawer. The three of us hoist up the spoon, slide it over the drawer's front panel, give it one last good shove, and send it sailing. It bounces and clinks a couple times when it hits the floor.

I look over at my two friends. "Now let's go save Gwindell!"

CHAPTER 34

"Many paws make light work."
—Isaiah

The three of us work the bowl of the spoon under the bar that's clamped down on Gwindell's leg and tail.

"Thank you, Isaiah," she says, her voice growing weaker.

"Don't thank me," I say. "This is a team effort."

"No mouse left behind," whispers Mikayla.

"Especially not my sister," says Gabriel, patting Gwindell's fur.

When the spoon is lodged between the bar and the wooden base of the mousetrap, Gabriel, Mikayla, Gilligan, Gordon, and I stand beneath the long handle.

"On my count," I say. "One, two, three—grab!"

The five of us jump as high as we can and catch hold of the spoon.

"And pull!" cries Gabriel.

The bar rises. But not enough.

We let go and drop to the floor. Gwindell groans. I can tell she won't last much longer.

"Again!" I say. "One, two, three—grab!"

We all leap up and dangle off the spoon handle again.

"And pull!" shouts Gabriel. "Harder! Come on! Give it everything you've got, guys!"

We're all grunting and groaning. Cheeks and faces are turning red. Except mine. I'm turning purple.

Gabriel gives a final, herculean yank and—hidey-ho!—my simple machine actually works. Our weight on the lever provides just enough force to pry up the bar.

And Gwindell has *just* enough strength left to roll sideways to freedom.

We did it!

Gabriel cradles his sister's head in his lap.

"My hero," Gwindell whispers with a faint smile.

"Shhh," says Gabriel. "We need to get you home."

We decide to abandon our food run and simply run as fast as we can.

For home.

CHAPTER 35

*"Words have no wings,
but they can fly a thousand miles."*
—Isaiah

B right and early the next morning, while the rest
of my new mischief sleeps off last night's party
to celebrate Gwindell's safe return, I scoot across the
street to visit my new human friend, Hailey.

No red-tailed hawks or cats pursue me, thank
goodness.

When I sneak into the house, I learn that, once
again, Hailey isn't going to school. Apparently, she is
sick a lot.

"Mostly," she tells me, "I'm sick of school. Plus, I
broke Mom's thermometer, so she can't tell if I *actually* have a fever or not."

"why don't you like school?" I ask with my feet. Fortunately, the question mark is very close to the shift key. Otherwise, I might not be able to ask Hailey anything.

"I like school," says Hailey. "Well, I used to. Then we moved here, and now going to school means sitting in the same room with a monster named Melissa."

"is she like a gorgon, the monstrous women with snakes on their head instead of hair, pointy tusks, and reptilian wings? i have read about those."

"No," Hailey says with a laugh. "Melissa is just a mean girl. She likes to call me Zit." She points to her hair. "Because I have a white head. Get it?"

"yes. very amusing."

"Um, not really. Whitehead is another name for a pimple, Isaiah."

I nod. I don't actually know what a pimple is. And, I suspect, I don't want to.

As we chat, I realize that Hailey and I have much in common. We both have our Horrible Places. Mine is the prison I shared with my family. Hers is the school where Melissa calls her mean names.

"Maybe tomorrow I'll go to school," says Hailey. "If Melissa calls me Zit again, I'll call her a Gorgon."

"if you do, you will be just like her."

She curls her lip. Makes a face. "Yeah. You've got a point, wise little mouse. I don't want *that* to happen..."

"me neither. one melissa seems to be enough."

"You hungry?"

I nod.

"Come on. There's crumb cake downstairs. You can have first dibs."

So we sit in the kitchen and chat over a delicious

breakfast. When she asks, I dance across the kitchen computer keyboard and tell Hailey the sad, awful truth about my life as a mouse:

"we mice are small and misunderstood. just about everybody and everything is bigger than we are. we go through life looking up at everything and being looked down on. not too many creatures seem to like us. except, of course, the ones that like to eat us. there are a lot of those. and humans? even though we have so much in common, most of them—present company excluded—don't treat us very nicely. that's my world, hailey. it really, truly is!"

I can't believe I typed all that without skipping a beat.

But Hailey? She sits there and listens. Well, actually, she reads, but you know what I mean. And when I finally finish, when I leap into an amazingly wide front and rear paw split just so I can type that final exclamation point, she sighs.

"I get what you're going through, Isaiah," she says. "Because I'm kind of going through some of the same stuff."

"thank goodness we have crumb cake."

"And double chocolate chip ice cream," Hailey adds with a laugh.

"and someplace safe with no melissas in it."

"Amen to that!"

From that day on, I visit Hailey whenever the sun is up and my adoptive mischief is snoozing.

I love our time together. Not just because Hailey sends me home every day with a napkin full of yummy-mummy goodies. What I really love about Hailey is that she listens. Even when I tell her about Mr. Brophy being the Mop Man and how I wish I could steal his keys and set my family free. She *listens*. I have never met any human, or mouse, quite like the white-haired Hailey.

Well, maybe Mikayla.

Mikayla's sweet and kind like Hailey. She might be a good listener, too.

She just doesn't like to listen to *me* all that much.

CHAPTER 36

"Our brightest blazes are often
kindled by unexpected sparks."
—Isaiah

B ack in the burrow with Mikayla's mischief, it seems I'm getting more and more respect.

Especially after I orchestrate what I call Operation Acorn.

One night, on our daily food run into the Brophys' house, I tell everybody to bring along as many acorns as they can carry. We haul them up to the countertops and chuck them like cannonballs at all the mousetraps we can see down below.

The spring-loaded traps leap across the kitchen floor like crazy once we trip them with our nut bombardment!

When the Brophys rush into the kitchen to see what's causing such a ruckus, I use the diversion to launch a sneak attack on their dining table. We dash across their abandoned plates (all of them heaped with food) and grab everything we can carry—in our paws as well as a pair of napkin sacks!

The next night, we grab a whole bag of Doritos (nacho cheese, naturally) we find hidden in Dwayne's bedroom. We have to rip the bag open with our teeth and carry the cheesy triangles, one by one, down the sink pipe hole, but it's a fun food run. We sing songs as we carry our cargo back to the burrow. I only wish Mikayla was with us. Perhaps she would've joined in on the chorus.

Then there's the trick I accidentally played on Mrs. Brophy. I don't want to go into details, but suffice it to say, it involved a bowl of chocolate-covered raisins and the fact that mouse droppings look a *lot* like chocolate-covered raisins.

"You could be a good leader, Isaiah," James the Wise tells me. "We know that you are different from all the other mice in our mischief. But your differences give you certain advantages: inventiveness, resourcefulness..."

"Blueness!" cracks Gabriel.

We all laugh. I am, after all, what James the Wise calls a "team player." This sort of good-natured ribbing is quite common in families. And when it comes to my adoptive family, I am quite willing to do anything and everything that needs to be done.

Except talk about my past.

That's personal.

And very, very private.

CHAPTER 37

"Silence is golden.
Old mice are gray."
—Isaiah

One night, James the Wise and the Council of Elders summon me to their high chamber.

It's time for *my* knees to start knocking together. The summons is very official-looking. Scary, even.

But not as scary as the chamber where the elders are staring at me stonily.

Why do the elders want to talk to me? I wonder. Did I do something wrong? Have they decided to kick me out of their mischief? Is it back to licking the bottoms of garbage barrels for me? What if I never see Mikayla again?

"Isaiah the Blue," booms one of the elders. "Step forward and hear your fate."

I do as I am told. I step forward to "hear my fate," which, by the way, is a very ominous thing for an elderly mouse to yell at you, and by *ominous*, I mean *not good*.

They're going to kick me out. I just know it. I'll be living in the gutter again.

James the Wise rises from his throne at the far end of the chamber. "Isaiah." His voice is strong and firm. "We, the elders of the Brophy Mischief, have taken a vote. Our verdict was unanimous."

Yep. Here it comes. The old heave-ho.

"You, Isaiah the Brave, are henceforth and forthwith hereby to be known, now and forevermore, as…"

I close my eyes.

"…a true son of this mischief!"

I gulp a little. They're not kicking me out; they're officially adopting me!

I feel a huge surge of relief and happiness that I'm not being kicked out of the mischief. *They like me!* And maybe this could prove to Mikayla that we can be accepted even if we *are* a little different, especially by our own family.

Family. My joy is dimmed by what I need to say now.

"Thank you for this high honor, elders," I say, bowing my head. "But I already have a family."

"Would you care to tell us about them?" a gray mouse named Griswold quickly asks. He's rubbing his paws together like he's eager to hear my story so he can blab about it to all his friends.

"No, sir. Not really."

"We're all quite curious," adds an ancient mouse with a very toothy smile. Her name is Grundle. She's lost all her whiskers and wears dark spectacles made out of discarded vanilla extract bottles.

"In our family," says Grundle, "we don't have any secrets. Tell us, Isaiah. What made you so different? What made you so…so…*blue*?"

My heart was sinking. Did they really want me for *me*, or for the amusement of having a strange blue mouse to tell tales about? I wasn't ready to share my painful past, especially to these old gossips.

Before I can speak up, James the Wise raises his paw. "Enough," he commands. "We *all* have secrets, Grundle. For instance, I know those aren't your real teeth. Those are two pieces of human chewing gum. Chiclets, I believe they are called."

Grundle quickly covers her mouth.

So do all the other elders—to stifle their giggles.

"If or when Isaiah is ready to tell us about his past," James the Wise continues, "he will tell us. For now, Isaiah the Brave, you are an honorary son of the Brophy Mischief. Welcome to your *new* family."

I feel honored.

And a little lonely, too.

All this talk about a "new" family is making me miss Abe and Winnie and my ninety-four other brothers and sisters even more.

It's been so long since the day I escaped. I've even given up on re-marking my scent trail. Maybe Benji will never plan another breakout.

Maybe I'll never see my "old" family ever again.

CHAPTER 38

"A mouse wrapped up in himself
makes a very small package."
—Isaiah

Later that same night, I go outside to gaze up at the glorious moon.

It's what I do when I'm feeling bluer than usual.

I heave a sad sigh. I miss my brothers and sisters so, so much. I remember them all, of course, but some more than others.

Abe, my red-furred brother. He was my best bud in the whole world and such a joker! If he were here with me, we'd be doing that chocolate raisin prank every night at the Brophy house.

And Winnie! I call her Winnie the Wonderful because—

Yipes!

I just heard something. A noise. In the shrubbery behind me.

Leaves rustling. Twigs snapping. The kind of sounds a cat might make if it were stealthily slinking through the underbrush, preparing to pounce on its prey!

Is it Lucifer? Is he on the prowl again? Am I the main course on his late-night dinner menu?

"Isaiah?"

I start breathing again. Right after I nearly jump out of my fur.

It's Mikayla.

"Don't do that!" I tell her.

"Do what?"

"Sneak up on me like that. You almost gave me a heart attack, and as I am a mouse, my heart is quite small. It wouldn't take much to attack it!"

"Don't be silly," she says. "You have a very big heart."

"No. It's mouse-sized. Teeny-tiny. Can't take too many more creatures stealthily sneaking up on it from the shadows."

"I wasn't sneaking!"

"You were slinking through the shrubbery."

Mikayla sighs. "I'm a mouse. It's what we do. We slink or we scurry. Sometimes we dart, but out here in the yard, it's mostly slinking."

I take a deep breath. Try to slow my rapidly pounding heart. It works. I no longer hear the tom-tom beat of war drums in my ears. "Sorry."

"You are forgiven, Isaiah. And when I said you had a big heart, I wasn't talking about its size. I meant that you are compassionate and kind. I've seen you in action. How you rescued Gwindell. The way you always make sure everybody else has enough to eat before you take a single bite…"

I don't know what to make of this.

Mikayla is talking to me. And rather sweetly, if

I do say so myself. Therefore, I have to wonder: did Grundle or Griswold or some other withered old elder tell her to grill me? Do they think that because I have a mouse crush on Mikayla, I'll reveal all my secrets to her, if not to them?

"Have you been sent out here to interrogate me?" I ask rather meanly.

Mikayla is confused. "To do what?"

"Quiz me. Ask me all sorts of questions about my past."

"No. I just came out for a walk. I love strolling in the moonlight and thought you might like it, too."

I feel bad for accusing Mikayla. "Oh."

"Well, *do* you like strolling in the moonlight?"

"Oh, yes. In fact, it's one of my favorite things to do. Moonlight strolling."

She smiles. "So why are we standing here?"

"Good point."

And so we stroll together. In the moonlight.

"So," I say, "are Grundle's teeth really made out of chewing gum?"

Mikayla laughs. "Yes. Gwindell found an entire box of spare teeth hidden under her mattress one morning when we were fluffing up the beds."

"No wonder she has such fresh, minty breath."

This time, we both laugh.

And then we talk. About everything and everybody—especially the Brophys. In fact, we're having such a grand time, I muster up some of my newfound courage to pop the question I've been longing to ask ever since that first day we met.

"Mikayla?"

"Yes, Isaiah?"

"Would you mind...I mean could you possibly... we're all alone out here..."

She smiles softly. "Would you like to hear me sing again?"

"More than all the cheese in the moon up above."

She looks around. "Well, since we *are* alone and no one would hear..." She opens her mouth, and as the first lovely note of her song begins to sound, there's a loud rustle as something huge leaps out of the shadows in front of us.

Lucifer.

CHAPTER 39

*"When the music changes,
so does the dance."*
—Isaiah

Mikayla and I leap behind a huge rock—the kind that would shatter a lawnmower blade if the Brophys ever cut their grass—and hunker down low.

But the cat isn't after us.

Tonight, it seems, he's going for some baby birds chirping in the leafy oak tree where I crash-landed into the hawk nest.

Wait a minute. Those chicks. Those are the very same baby hawks I met when their mother delivered me for breakfast.

Up in the trees, Lucifer is swatting at the chicks.

Batting their fuzzy noggins with the soft pad of his paw.

"He's playing Cat and Mouse with them," I mutter.

"But they're birds," whispers Mikayla.

"It doesn't matter what he bops. To an evil thing like Lucifer, life is one cruel game of Cat and Mouse."

"They're just babies," said Mikayla. "They can't defend themselves."

"Where's their mother when we actually need her?" I mumble. I hear another squawk. Lucifer just swatted another fuzzy head.

Once again, I can't believe I'm about to do what I'm about to do.

"Wait here," I say to Mikayla. "Hide." I stand up.

"What? Isaiah? What do you think you're doing?"

"Something I'm apparently very good at: acting like somebody else's dinner!" I zip out from the darkness and find a bright pool of moonlight. "Yoo-hoo? Baldy! Over here!"

Lucifer stops batting the baby birdies. Glares down at me with glowing yellow eyes.

"You look like a wrinkled prune!" I call.

"No he doesn't," says Mikayla, who, all of a sudden, is standing right beside me. "He looks like a plucked turkey!"

"Um, Mikayla," I say out of the corner of my mouth, "I thought you were going to hide and—"

"You thought wrong."

Lucifer interrupts us with a horrible hiss. In a flash, he abandons the chicks and comes charging down the tree after us.

"Fly, birds, fly!" I scream as I grab Mikayla's paw so we can run away. "Fly!"

"They might not be able to fly!" says Mikayla as we round the corner of the house with Lucifer in hot pursuit. "They're just babies!"

"Well, they need to learn! Fast!"

Lucifer is right on our tails. The cat is extremely fast.

He gains an inch or two on us every time we circle the house.

Panting, I tell Mikayla, "We should split up. He'll come after me, and I have treadmill training."

"Then why are you almost out of breath?" she gasps.

"Because we've run around this house six times..."

"We stay together," she says. "We're family."

"Well, that doesn't mean we have to die together..." But I can tell it's no use. Mikayla won't abandon me. It's very noble of her.

It may also be very unwise. Because Lucifer *is* going to catch us.

I've done the math in my head. Halfway through the next lap around the Brophy house, Lucifer will be in striking range. The lap after that, he'll snag us both.

He's going to kill us.

And eat us.

Right after he tortures us for a few hours.

The only good news? Well, the second I check in to mouse heaven, Mikayla will be there with me. They'll give her an angel robe and a harp, and ask her to sing in the choir.

It gives me something to look forward to after all the torturing, killing, and dying.

Suddenly, there's a screech behind us.

A *hawk* screech.

Mommy's back.

And now Mikayla and I have *two* killers chasing after us!

CHAPTER 40

"Faith gives one the ability to not panic."
—Isaiah

The red-tailed hawk swoops down.

I squeeze Mikayla's paw and wait for the pain of that sharp beak snatching me up again.

But it doesn't come. I hear a yowl and throw a desperate glance behind me as I keep running.

The hawk is attacking Lucifer!

She yanks him off the ground, zooms skyward, and opens her claws. Lucifer drops like a ton of bald bricks!

Of course, cats are very good at landing. They have an unusually flexible backbone

and are born with a "righting reflex" so they have the ability to reorient their bodies as they fall and land on their feet.

Which Lucifer does with a yelp.

The hawk dropped him over the driveway, which is made out of concrete and full of pebbly potholes. Lucifer landed right inside one.

While he's hissing at the moon, I lead Mikayla across the street and into Hailey's backyard.

"W-w-what is this p-p-place?" asks Mikayla, her voice shaky. I suspect she may not have traveled as widely as she once told me she had.

"We'll be safe in this house," I say as we bound up the steps toward the back door.

"Do humans live here?"

"Yes."

"Then we won't be safe!"

"Yes, we will. This human is different." We hop through the pet door. "Upstairs," I whisper.

"I'm afraid," says Mikayla as we tiptoe up the hall.

"There's no need to fear," I tell her. "My friend Hailey is very sweet."

"Really? And exactly when did a human and a

mouse, mortal enemies since forever, become friends?"

"Oh, about a week ago. We met over crumb cake."

We traipse across the floor and scale Hailey's bed-side table. It's late, so she's sound asleep. I politely sit on top of her alarm clock and wait for her to wake up. Mikayla hides behind it.

"I don't see how you could ever be friends with a human," Mikayla whispers from her hiding place. "They hate us!"

"Well," I say, pausing to reflect on the matter, "I suppose I could be friends with just about anyone—provided, of course, they wanted to be friends with *me*."

"You're strange, Isaiah."

"Thank you. But I prefer the term *different*."

Hailey yawns, opens an eye. Mikayla gasps and ducks behind the clock.

"Hello, Isaiah," Hailey says sleepily.

Since there is no keyboard handy, I just smile and wave.

"Who's your pretty friend?" she asks as Mikayla peeks over the top of the clock. "Any friend of Isaiah's is a friend of mine," Hailey tells her.

Now it's Mikayla's turn to smile and wave, but she does it much more timidly than me.

"You guys hungry?" Hailey swings her legs out of the bed and slips her feet into some very fluffy-looking half-shoes. "Let's see what's in the kitchen. My mom brought home cream horns from the bakery…"

Mikayla pops up from her hiding place.

Hailey just said the magic words.

CHAPTER 41

*"Words have no muscles,
but they are strong enough to break a heart."*
—Isaiah

While Mikayla feasts on her midnight snack, Hailey and I chat.

I suspect that Mikayla finds my keyboard dancing to be further proof of my peculiarity. After all, she can't read the words I am typing on the screen. Then again, she may not even be watching me. She has an entire cream horn to devour and has buried her face inside its frosting.

"how's school?" I ask.

"Better, I guess. Whenever Melissa calls me Zit, I just laugh at her."

"good for you."

"And I have a pretty cool English teacher, Mr. Randall. He likes reading books almost as much as I do. How about you, Isaiah? If you can write, I'm guessing you can read. Either that or you're just a very talented tap dancer who has no idea what all this gobbledygook on the screen says!"

That makes me laugh. So my next sentence *is* gobbledygook. I quickly compose myself, however, and compose a quick verse:

"i like books, i really do. books with stories and pictures, too. books of mice and things that grow. books about hailey, who I am happy to know!"

I do another split to hit that exclamation point, but it's worth it.

When Mikayla finishes as much of her cream horn as she can stuff into her stomach, Hailey packs up the rest in a clear plastic bag. She also gives us an entire package of something called string cheese.

"Be sure you guys peel off the plastic before you eat it," she advises.

"and this cheese is made from string instead of milk?" I ask.

"No, it's just stringy, but they couldn't call it

stringy cheese or people might think it's made out of boogers."

"what's a booger?"

"Never mind. Come on. I'll give you two a ride home so you don't have to worry about bumping into Lucifer again."

She stows our goody bags in the front pocket of her hoody. Then she bends down to the table so Mikayla and I can hop into the hood. The soft cotton lining makes for a very cozy carriage ride.

"She's very nice," says Mikayla, as gravity causes us to snuggle together down in the peak of the hood. "The nicest human person I've ever met."

"I concur. She's different from most of her species."

We lean back and bask in the moonlight as we gently sway back and forth. It's like riding home in a comfy hammock.

Mikayla sighs contentedly. She is very happy, I can tell. We're snug and warm and safe.

"Mikayla?" I say. "Would you mind if I sang to you? After all, it is customary for boys to sing to girls, especially girls they've developed a certain fondness for..."

Maybe I really have become Isaiah the Brave. I can't believe I just said that.

"I'd love to hear you sing," says Mikayla, her breath as sweet as apple pie.

And so I sing my very best mouse song.

One thing I forgot to mention: all those talents I possess may have crowded out some of the other talents I might have if I were a typical, normal mouse. For instance, singing. I'm pretty bad at it.

"Enough," she says, laughing, after a few sour notes. "My turn!"

Then, right there in Hailey's hoody, Mikayla sings for me!

It's ultrasonic, so Hailey can't hear it, but I sure can—it's loud and resonating, but sweet and emotional at the same time. The lyrics are simple. All about the moonlight and how it makes young mice under its spell fall in love, and how love is all that really matters.

It's heavenly.

Even better than warm apple pie.

CHAPTER 42

*"Fall down seven times,
stand up eight."*
—Isaiah

The very next night, we're both singing a different tune.

Lucifer is chasing after us again, this time *inside* the house.

Mikayla, Gabriel, Gulliver, and I make up one scavenging squad on the nightly food hunt.

And, of course, Mikayla and I are the ones Lucifer is gunning for. I think he remembers my blue fur from the previous evening. And perhaps he memorized her curly tail because, after all, he was behind us during that mad dash around and around the house.

There are ten other four-mouse teams racing

around inside the Brophy home this evening because, earlier in the day, our spies discovered that the family would be going out to dinner at an all-you-can-eat Chinese buffet. That meant their cupboards, pantry, and secret stashes of bedroom food would be left unguarded.

James the Wise ordered a full-scale home invasion. We were anticipating coming back to the burrow with enough food to last a month. After Gwindell's encounter with the mousetrap, a lot of mice were afraid of going on food runs every night, so tonight's haul was important for our mischief.

We were not anticipating running into Lucifer again. Or that he would be so extremely clever.

By chasing us into a bathroom, he has us cornered. The sides of the bathtub are too slippery for us to climb, so we can't tunnel out through the drainpipe. The cat is near the sink, close to the door. In that position, he's blocking the exit *and* our access to the sink's escape pipe.

We have no choice but to hide behind the toilet.

Lucifer hunkers down and grins. I can read the thoughts behind his grim yellow eyes: "I can wait *all night*."

"This is it," says Gulliver. "We're goners!"

"Take it easy, soldier," says Gabriel.

"How can I take it easy? He has us trapped! Trapped, I tell you!"

Gulliver might be correct.

The nefarious Lucifer is laying siege to us. A siege is a military strategy where your enemy surrounds you, cuts off your avenue of retreat, and blocks your supply routes. It leaves you without essentials, such as food and water, eventually forcing you to surrender.

Unless, of course, you've also studied military tactics!

As it happens, I once read a book about the strategies of the famous French warrior Napoléon Bonaparte, who led thirty-four battles between 1792 and 1815, of which he lost only six, an excellent record. Napoléon's battle strategy was all about rapid movement by an overwhelming number of troops.

Mice are fast.

And there were already forty-four of us in the house.

Soon, there could be more. An army large enough to scare off even the most monstrous cat.

I turn to Mikayla. "We need you to sing the Battle Call of the Mice! Sing it as loudly as you did last night—we need every able-bodied member of the mischief to come storming into this bathroom!"

"But I've already told you, Isaiah," says Gabriel. "Mikayla can't sing. She's a girl."

"Oh, yes, I can," Mikayla says firmly. "Better than any boy."

I nod, agreeing. She was more suited for this job than any male mouse I've ever heard sing.

"Impossible," says Gulliver.

"Nothing's impossible," says Mikayla. "Some of us are just, well, *different*. Stand back, boys!"

Mikayla takes in a deep breath, and when she lets it out, her voice soars far and wide. The battle call is a song that every mouse knows, whether they grew up in a burrow or a Horrible Place. It isn't sung very often, but it has an immense, incredible effect.

Lucifer's eyes get as big as Oreos. His ears are pretty big and pointy. He's definitely picking up on Mikayla's energetic ultrasonic vibrations.

"Wow!" says Gabriel. "You sing the battle call better than any mouse I've ever heard."

"Louder, too," says Gulliver, covering his ears. "They could probably hear you all the way down in the basement—of the house next door."

"That was the plan," I say, tucking my paw under some belly fur so I can sort of look like Napoléon.

And guess what? Napoléon was right.

Very soon, terrified by our overwhelming number of troops, Lucifer does what all those armies who lost to Napoléon did.

He runs and hides.

CHAPTER 43

"A cat bitten by a snake
dreads even rope."
—Isaiah

"**Y**ou should have seen that mean cat scat,"
I type on the laptop computer in Hailey's bedroom.

Mikayla and I are back for another visit and, hopefully, another hoody ride home.

Red Boy, Hailey's cat, hops up into Hailey's lap
and raises its hindquarters, commanding Hailey to
rub the magic spot in front of his tail.

Mikayla gasps when the cat makes its entrance.

"Don't worry," says Hailey. "Red Boy just needs

a little loving. He's not interested in eating you. He likes salmon and tuna and those cat treats shaped like fish."

Mikayla turns to me. "Everything in this house is so different, including the cat."

"Yes," I say to her. "Isn't different wonderful?"

"What are you two gabbing about?" asks Hailey, because she can't hear our words.

I start typing again.

"we were discussing how lucifer has been defeated...at least for now. maybe he won't mess with our mischief anymore. no one wants to fight when the odds are 1,000 to 1 against you."

"You're something else, Isaiah," says Hailey. "Who knew you were such a great field commander? Tomorrow, to celebrate, I'll bring you a napoleon."

"is napoleon still alive?" I had to ask.

"Nope. A napoleon is a pastry. Sort of like the cream horn, only with custard in the middle and chocolate on top."

Mikayla is beaming. She is also drooling.

"mikayla deserves a reward like that," I type. "she is the one who belted out the battle call so brilliantly.

we had mice joining us from houses up and down the block. even the ones from your cellar."

"We have mice?"

"if you have a cellar, hailey, you have mice."

She shrugs. "I don't mind. Maybe one of them will be heroic like you. Mice have been famous throughout history, you know."

"you mean human history? because mouse history has nothing in it but mice..."

Hailey laughs. "Yes. Human history. Do you know that the Greek god Apollo was called Lord of Mice? And then there's the mouse that the elephant-headed Hindu god Ganesha rides—at least in pictures."

She shows me a picture of an elephant person riding a mouse, and all I can think is, *That poor mouse.*

Hailey keeps going with her list of famous mice.

"There's Mickey Mouse, Mighty Mouse, Jerry, Speedy Gonzales, and Stuart Little. And of course, in my opinion, the most heroic mice are the ones who've saved so many lives in research laboratories—"

Yipes!

The mere mention of the L-word sends me into a panic. I jump off the laptop, race across the computer desk, and run as fast as I can.

Right out Hailey's window.

CHAPTER 44

*"Rocks need no protection from the rain.
I wish I were a rock."*
—Isaiah

From the window, I slide down the drainpipe.

Dash across the yard.

Crash into the woods.

I keep running until I find a snug nook in the roots of a towering tree, where I curl up into a ball.

And then I let myself do something I've been holding back from doing ever since I lost my original mischief.

I cry.

I let the tears empty out all the pain and loneliness I've been keeping bottled up inside.

Have you ever lost your whole family?

All in one fell swoop?

I certainly hope not.

If you had, you would know how much it hurts. And why I just need to hug myself and cry.

"Oh, poor Abe, poor Winnie, poor Benji, Hezekiah, Maria, Rudolpho, and Zeke," I sob. "I got out, but you're still trapped in the Horrible Place. Being tortured in the...the lab!"

I say the L-word.

I say it out loud.

It makes my limbs shiver and my tail shake. Oh, the nightmares I could tell you about what goes on in the lab. What they do to us mice should be illegal. Perhaps it is illegal, but the Long Coats at the lab don't care—they do it anyway.

Uh-oh. I hear noises.

Rustling in the underbrush.

This can't be good. It might be Lucifer, seeking revenge.

Worse, it might be Mr. Brophy, come to take me back to the lab, where he works as a Mop Man and Key Keeper.

I curl up tighter, close my eyes. I've never felt more lost or alone.

"Isaiah? Are you okay?"

I open one eye. It's Gabriel. Gwindell, Gilligan, and Godfrey are with him.

A new voice calls, "Isaiah, where are you?"

It's Hailey.

In a flash, the other mice scurry under leaf piles to hide. Gabriel helps Gwindell crouch behind a pine-cone.

"It's okay, you guys," says Mikayla, climbing out of Hailey's hoody to stand on her shoulder. "This human is different."

The other mice are shocked into a momentary silence.

"Wow," says Gabriel, finally. "Her fur is white as snow. The good kind of snow. Before the dogs get to it."

"Isn't she beautiful?" says Mikayla. "She's as nice as she is pretty."

"Stunning," says Gwindell. "Her eyes are amazing. They blaze with icy fire!"

Hailey, of course, can't hear all of the mouse chatter. She kneels down in the dirt to talk to me. I notice that she's brought along her laptop.

"Are you okay?" she asks.

I nod to let her know that, physically, I'm fine.

A tear trickles down my cheek. I must confess, I am quite touched that all these creatures genuinely care about me. They'd risk the danger of the yard at night to rescue me? Maybe I'm not as alone in this world as I thought.

"I did some quick research," says Hailey. She opens up her computer. Shows me the screen. "Is this where you used to live, Isaiah?"

"It's where Mr. Brophy works," Hailey continues. "And it's not very far from here…"

I look into her crystal-blue eyes. I look at my friends. I look at Mikayla.

It's time.

I take a deep breath.

And then I tell them my story.

CHAPTER 45

*"When writing the story of your life,
don't let anyone else dance on the keyboard."*
—Isaiah

I step up on the laptop so I can tell my tale to every-body, Hailey included.

While I type, I also recite what I'm writing.

"yes. the lamina research lab was the only home i had ever known until mikayla so graciously invited me into the brophy mischief."

"We love having you with us, Isaiah," says Gabriel.

"None of us has ever eaten so well!" adds Gwindell.

"Or scared off Lucifer, the devil cat," says Mikayla.

"thank you. i have enjoyed my time with you all. you, too, hailey. especially when i compare my new life to my old. at the lab, the horrible place, they conducted countless experiments on me and my family. they did this to us because they could. they were big, we were small. in the human world, might makes right. the strong oppress the weak."

"Same thing's true in middle school," says Hailey. "But some of us try to be different."

"you, hailey, are the most remarkably different human i have ever met. if only there were more like you."

"Maybe there are, and we just haven't met them yet," says Hailey.

"we can hope. anyway, at the lab, they made me to be very, very different. i think they gave me a bigger brain. superior intelligence. i suspect that is why i can read and learn big words and do all the other things i can do. they also made me blue so i'd be easy to identify. same with my brothers and sisters. they gave us all very distinctive colors. because they could. they never asked our permission for anything they wanted to do. they just did it. because they could."

"How long did this go on?" asks Hailey.

"my whole life. finally, one day, we decided enough

was enough. my big brother, benji, who is ten times braver than i could ever be, came up with an escape plan. you see, mr. brophy likes to prop open the rear door when he mops. the breeze dries the floor so he doesn't have to. mr. brophy is extremely lazy. benji said we should make a run for it the next time mr. brophy mopped the floor."

"Were you in cages?" asks Hailey.

"yes, but not the kind with bars. our jail cells were more like plastic boxes. very similar to the sealed containers the brophys use for storing leftovers in their refrigerator."

"Those are easy enough to chew through," says Gabriel. "If you have time."

"exactly."

"Exactly what?" asks Hailey, who couldn't hear Gabriel's question.

"we could chew through the plastic walls of our prison cells. benji said, first thing in the morning, we should all nibble a hole in the floor and then cover it up with cedar shavings. and since the long coats had made us all so very special..."

"You have very sharp teeth," says Hailey.

I nod. "like razors. what would take an ordinary mouse several days, we could chew through in an hour. we did it on the morning of the jailbreak."

"So, Mr. Brophy propped open the back door, you guys chewed holes in your plastic cages, and you hightailed it out of there?"

"yes. we ran out the back door. we scattered in ninety-seven different directions so the long coats couldn't catch us all. i hid in a sewer drain and tightroped my way on a power line over an alley strewn with rusty barrels that smelled like rotten eggs."

"This is so awesome," says Hailey. "You guys did it. You escaped!"

I shake my head. "no. i am the only one who made it this far. the others were all captured and taken back to the lab where, i'm sure, they are now kept in steel cages, the kind with bars you can't nibble through. they are prisoners. i am the only one who is free."

Gabriel and Gwindell drop their heads and say a silent prayer for my lost family.

Mikayla sings a haunting dirge. The sort of sad song you might hear at a funeral. She repeats the same refrain:

Dear Mouse God,
may our brothers and sisters find freedom,
may they find peace,
may they one day be released.

As Mikayla sings, I realize something. My brothers and sisters aren't able to "find" freedom. They can't "find" peace. And they'll never be released by anyone who works for Lamina Research Lab.

No, if I want Mikayla's beautiful words to come true, there's only one way to make it happen.

And just like that, it hits me.

I know what I have to do.

I know how to rescue my family!

CHAPTER 46

"The best-laid plans of mice and men
might actually work."
—Isaiah

Early the next morning, just before sunrise, I join Hailey up in her room.

From the window, I have an excellent view of the Brophys' house and, more important, their driveway.

Hailey stayed up all night doing research on her computer.

"I had to do some digging, but I found an article about the local Lamina Lab, a leader in genetic engineering, being investigated by Humans for Animals."

I hop onto the keyboard.

"are there really people like that? humans who care how mice are treated?" I ask.

"Sure. Lots of us. Anyway, HFA did an undercover investigation at this one Lamina Lab. But when they alerted the local authorities and the cops raided the place, 'there were no mice or other animals present in the lab' according to this article."

"picnic day."

"Huh?"

"one day, last spring, the long coats put us all in portable cages and took us for a ride to a quiet place in the forest where the trees were very tall and smelled like floor cleaner. they put our cages on long wooden tables, tossed cheese into our crates, and called it a 'picnic.' when one of the long coats received a telephone call advising him that 'the coast was clear,' we were hauled back to the lab."

"This raid I read about took place back in the spring. Early May."

I nod and type, "picnic day."

"But even if the police had found you guys, mice and rats aren't protected under the federal Animal Welfare Act like dogs, cats, and rabbits are."

"why not? if you prick us, do we not bleed? if you tickle us, do we not laugh? if you poison us, do we not die?"

"That's from Shakespeare, right?"

"indeed. mr. shakespeare was one human who definitely understood how it feels to be a mouse."

At precisely 7:05 a.m., I spy Mr. Brophy waddling out of his house and heading to his pickup truck. He's carrying a very large paper sack. I'm guessing it's his lunch bag.

"what day is this?" I ask Hailey.

"Monday. I have school…"

"and mr. brophy, the mop man, has work. i think we can safely assume that he goes to the lamina labs every morning at approximately the same time."

"Yeah. I usually hear his truck pulling out at around

seven. Right before my mom comes into my room to wake me up."

There's a rap of knuckles on the door.

I run for cover. But the door is already creaking open.

So I strike a pose on Hailey's bookshelf, next to her collection of odd plastic dolls.

Her mother steps into the room.

"Hailey? Time to…oh. You're already up?"

"Yeah."

"Excited about school?"

"You bet."

"Well, that's good to hear. I'll go fix you your breakfast. I think we still have some crumb cake."

"Um, if it's okay, I'm more in the mood for oatmeal," she says, because we devoured the last crumb of the crumb cake last night.

"Oatmeal it is."

Her mom leaves the room. I dash back to the keyboard.

"tonight, when mr. brophy returns home, we need to determine how much cargo room there is in the covered bed of his pickup truck."

"Why?" says Hailey.

"it is time for another napoleonic invasion. this time, we're taking our mouse army to the horrible place. the lab."

CHAPTER 47

"Beware of big wooden horses."
—Isaiah

M onday night, after the food run, Gabriel and I go on a scouting mission.

We scurry along the edge of the driveway, then scale the muddy tires and dented sides of Mr. Brophy's truck. We peer through the windows of the structure covering the rear end of the vehicle.

"Wowzers," says Gabriel. "You could easily fit a thousand, maybe two thousand mice in this little rolling room."

"Such is my plan," I say. "We put together a massive mouse army and hide in the back of Mr. Brophy's pickup. We go with him to the lab, and when we're safely through the security gates, we storm the castle!"

"The lab is in a castle?"

"It's a metaphor."

"Oh. I've heard of those. They taste good."

I shake my head and move on. "This pickup truck will be just like the Trojan horse."

"Um, is that another metaphor?"

"Actually, it's more of a simile. It means that we will launch a sneak attack in much the same manner as the Greeks who attacked the city of Troy."

"What did they do?"

"The Greeks built a huge, hollow wooden horse with a few soldiers hidden inside, then the rest of the army pretended to sail away. The Trojans thought the surrendering Greeks left the wooden horse as a gift, so they brought it behind their city walls. That night, while the Trojans celebrated their victory, those Greek soldiers crept out of the wooden horse, opened the city gates, and the rest of the Greek army came storming in. They destroyed Troy and ended the Trojan War!"

"Are we going to destroy the lab?"

"No. We're just going to set my family free."

Of course, for my plan to work, I needed mice. Lots and lots of mice.

So Gabriel and I scuttle back to the burrow and tell the whole mischief our plan.

In the great hall under the floorboards, I address the mass of eager mice. "My friends! We will use the same tactics that we used to defeat Lucifer in the Battle of the Bathroom," I say. "Overwhelming numbers. A swift strike. The instant Mr. Brophy unlocks the lab door, one thousand, no, *two* thousand mice will race out of the back of his truck and storm into the building. My friends, always remember—we have the 'eek' factor on our side. What happens the second a human sees a mouse?"

"They shriek 'eek'!" answers Mikayla.

"And jump up on a chair," adds Gwindell.

"Well," I say, "imagine how loudly they'll shriek and how high they'll jump when they see *thousands* of us. A vast, roiling army of furry, whiskered soldiers!"

I'm really whipping the crowd up.

Well, *most* of them.

Grundle, the disgruntled elder with the fake buckteeth, is glowering at me. She raises her paw. The crowd goes silent.

"We do not, as a rule, risk our lives for strangers," she says, sniffing with disdain.

"They're not strangers," I say. "They're my family."

"Perhaps," says Grundle. "But they are not *our* family."

I feel my whiskers droop. "But I can't do any of this without all of you…"

"Then, little boy blue, you shan't be doing it. Now then, children, kindly disperse. I believe you've all heard quite enough from your so-called brother."

"Wait a second," shouts Gabriel, jumping up beside me on my matchbox. "Do I have to remind everyone that this mischief has sacred words we live by? 'No mouse left behind!' Well, Isaiah has more than honored those words."

"Indeed he has," adds Gwindell, hobbling forward on her crutches. "Even when others were ready to abandon them."

"And," says Gabriel, "I should also remind the elders that you made Isaiah an honorary son of this mischief not too long ago." Gabriel puts a paw up to his mouth so he can whisper to me. "Show them your medallion."

"Um, I forgot where I put it…"

Fortunately, this is when James the Wise rises from his soap-bar throne.

"What Gabriel says is true. Isaiah *is* our son and brother. Therefore, his family is our family. The ancient edict applies: Leave no mouse behind! Go, all of you, and rescue our imprisoned brothers and sisters!"

"We leave at dawn!" I cry. "Who's coming with me?"

Every able-bodied mouse in the burrow shouts, "Me!"

Hearing those wonderful words, I've never felt less alone in my life!

CHAPTER 48

*"With a stout heart,
a mouse can lift an elephant."*
—Isaiah

Mikayla sings for me again.

Well, it's not exactly for *me*...she sings the Battle Call of the Mice to summon all our cousins to the cause. But I'm there to hear it, and trust me, it is *be-yoo-ti-ful*.

Mice come trooping into the burrow from every house up and down the block.

"Grab some cheese, fellas," says my first lieutenant, Gabriel, greeting our neighbors. "And help yourself to Dwayne's Doritos. It's going to be a long night. We move out at first light."

After midnight, there is a steady stream of fresh recruits marching out of the basement, down the driveway, and up into the back of Mr. Brophy's truck. Fortunately, there is one window on the truck cap that Mr. Brophy should've replaced years ago with something stronger than a sheet of cardboard and duct tape. It's easy for the mouse brigade to slip, one by one, through the crack and drop down to the soiled mattress covering the rusty truck bed.

Hailey lends a hand, loading her backpack and

hoody with mice, ferrying them to the pickup. It's a big help, because the hawk wouldn't dare attack us with a human so close by.

As for Lucifer, he doesn't interfere with our movements because he has become the ultimate scaredy-cat. He must sense the vast army of mice gathering in the underbelly of his home. That's why he's spending the night curled up tight on top of his cat tree.

When the entire truck bed is jammed with mice, Hailey comes over from her house with a tube of rolled-up netting.

"I found this in the garage. Dad puts it up in the backyard so we can play volleyball. But if you guys use it to make a couple of hammocks in the truck bed, you could fit in triple your troops."

I nod enthusiastically.

"Just make sure you return it," she says. "I want to play volleyball this weekend. I think I could actually beat you, Isaiah. I have the height advantage."

We both smile.

Around three in the morning, I climb up the side of the pickup to inspect my massive invasion force. Thanks to Hailey's netting, Mikayla's singing, and the courage of all the mice in Suburbia, we are *five thousand strong!*

I'm about to hop in and join the army when Gabriel taps me on the shoulder.

"I've been thinking," he says. "One of us needs to go into the lab with Mr. Brophy and give an ultrasonic signal when the back door is propped open. We can't really attack until he does that."

He's right. "I'll do it," I say.

"Are you sure? Because I'm willing to volunteer…"

I shake my head. "No, Gabriel. It's my mischief. My old home. I know my way around inside the lab."

"You could probably sneak into the lab riding inside his shirt pocket."

"Or the back pocket of his pants," I say.

"Bad idea. You don't want Mr. Brophy sitting on you."

"Good point. We'll go with the shirt."

Now I just have to figure out a way to climb across Mr. Brophy's chest and into his pocket without his noticing me.

I'm good, but am I *that* good?

CHAPTER 49

*"Given a challenge, be like the sun:
Rise to the occasion."*
—Isaiah

I'm napping in the truck's cup holder when I hear footsteps and grumbling.

"You need to buy more, Luanne. Today! We're down to one snack pack!"

Oh, no! I must've dozed off. Mr. Brophy is coming down the walkway. Heading for the cab of his truck.

Where I'm sitting with my electric-blue fur in plain sight.

His hand is on the door.

If he sees me, our invasion will be over before it's even launched!

Thinking fast, I scoot up and hide in the crack where the seat cushion meets the padded seat back. I'm right behind the seat-belt buckle when Mr. Brophy swings open the door and slides behind the wheel. He drops a brown paper bag in the passenger seat, turns the ignition key, and backs out of the driveway.

We're on our way!

After a few minutes of rumbling down the road, I smell something foul. Like rotten eggs.

No, it's not Mr. Brophy or what he had for breakfast.

We must be close to that alleyway strewn with toxic-waste barrels that I crossed over during the high-wire-act portion of my escape. That means we're getting close to the Horrible Place. Lamina Labs. I need to make my move and climb into Mr. Brophy's pocket.

Quietly, very quietly, I slip out of my hiding place.

My plan is to carefully work my way up the passenger-side seat, tiptoe over to Mr. Brophy's shoulder, slide down the front of his work shirt, and crawl into his front right pocket, which I can see in the pickup truck's rearview mirror.

Which means Mr. Brophy will be able to see me sliding into his pocket, too!

Okay. I need a new plan.

While I'm thinking, I glance in the truck's side-view mirror.

Well, hidey-ho and what do you know?

It's Hailey. She's following Mr. Brophy's pickup truck on her bicycle!

Mr. Brophy's arm reaches across the front seat. His hand disappears inside the brown paper sack.

I jump back and, arms spread wide, freeze against the cab's rear window.

"Where's my ding-dang pickled egg?"

He finds what he's looking for. Plucks it out of the bag. And jams the slick white ball into his mouth.

This is not only grossing me out, it is giving me an idea.

I can hide inside his lunch bag instead of his shirt pocket. No way is Mr. Brophy going into the lab without his beloved Doritos. It's easy for me to slide down the seat cushion and slink into the sack. I work my way underneath the chip bag without crinkling the plastic wrapper.

The truck comes to a stop.

"Morning, Brophy," says a voice outside the cab.

"Morning, Tom."

We must be at the security gate.

"Who's this kid on the bike behind you?" asks Tom the guard.

"I don't know," says Mr. Brophy. "Never seen her before in my life."

"Could be another one of those Humans for Animals nuts," says Tom. "I better take care of it. Have a good one."

"You too, Tom."

We're moving again. Now it feels like we're backing up. Swerving left.

The truck bumps into something. We bounce and rock. I hear the ultrasonic squeak of five thousand startled mice behind me.

"Stupid loading dock," grumbles Mr. Brophy. "Why'd they have to put it there?"

He shuts off the truck's engine and grabs his lunch sack. I'm swaying back and forth, bumping into another one of those slimy pickled eggs.

Now I can tell we're walking up steps. We reach a plateau. This must be the flat slab of concrete I leapt off of when I ran out the back door.

Winnie and Abe and Benji are only twenty, maybe thirty, feet away, on the other side of a thick steel door.

I hear keys jingling. We're going in!

CHAPTER 50

*"If a cat wants a fish
it has to get its paws wet."*
—Isaiah

I'm dropped on a metal surface of some sort. I peek out of my bag.

I'm inside Mr. Brophy's janitor closet. I can see his rolling bucket and his jugs and canisters of cleaning chemicals.

"Mr. Brophy?" says a familiar voice outside the closet. "Might I see you for a moment?"

"Sure, Dr. Ledbetter," says Mr. Brophy. "Right away, sir."

I hear Mr. Brophy's shoes squeak and his key ring jingle as he leaves. I crawl out of the lunch bag, drop down to the floor, and lean around the doorjamb to spy on Mr. Brophy and the Long Coat named Dr. Ledbetter.

"Please be advised, Mr. Brophy, that we are at a heightened state of alert and have activated the alarms on all the windows and doors, including the one behind me. The one, I am told, you like to prop open when you mop this floor."

"It's for the mice," says Mr. Brophy. "I figure the fresh air might do them good."

"Be that as it may, this door and all others in the facility are to remain locked tight until shift change at three."

Uh-oh.

If Mr. Brophy doesn't prop open the back door, how is my five-thousand-mouse army going to storm into the building?

Will I have to free my family all by myself?

And even if I can manage to do that, how are all ninety-seven of us going to escape if every door or window we try to open will trigger an alarm?

"No problem, Professor," Mr. Brophy tells Dr. Ledbetter. "But if you don't mind me asking, why all the fuss?"

"The security guard at the main gate just advised me that he encountered an animal rights activist attempting to gain access to this facility."

"That girl on the bicycle?"

"We suspect she is a spy. Do *not*, under any circumstances, open this door."

"No, sir, Professor."

Mr. Brophy tugs on a key with a sort of squarish black plastic head. The key, and about a dozen others sharing the ring with it, are attached to his belt by an extendable cable.

I watch as he slips the key into the lock and gives it a firm twist.

Some rescue mission this turned out to be. I'm trapped. Locked inside the Horrible Place again, and my mouse army has no way of getting inside.

I need to find Benji. He'll know what to do.

When Mr. Brophy isn't looking, I slip out of the closet and sneak down to the room where they kept me and my entire family locked up in those plastic boxes.

But the boxes have all been replaced by rolling racks of metal cages.

"Benji?" I whisper.

No answer.

"Abe? Winnie?"

Nothing. Maybe they're all napping, exhausted from another round of research experiments.

I ladder up the closest rack of prison cells to take a closer look.

Oh, no.

The cages are empty.

My family is gone.

CHAPTER 51

*"Necessity is the mother of invention.
But she's not a very nice mommy."*
—Isaiah

I don't know what to do!

My family is gone. Disappeared. Maybe they're all dead.

Or maybe they've all been shipped off to another Lamina Lab for different kinds of experiments. That article Hailey found said there were Lamina Labs all over the state—all over the country!

I need to think. Think, think, think.

Okay. The doors to *this* Lamina Lab are securely locked. My entire army of five thousand mice is stranded outside in a rusty pickup truck, and I'm basically a prisoner again.

Yipes!

Remember that nasty guard dog I told you about? The one whose bark I imitated to startle Lucifer?

He's sniffing his way down the row of cages, following my scent.

He spots me. But he doesn't bark and sound the alarm. He just growls and shows me his shiny fangs.

The Doberman thinks he can scare me back into my cage, even though I don't really have one anymore.

I decide to give him a taste of his own medicine, so to speak.

I bark just like he would!

The guard dog is stunned. Confused. I seize my moment and take off.

I zip out of the cage room and race down the nearest hall. It will only take the guard dog a few seconds to recover from his shock. I need to find a safe hiding place. Fast.

I round a corner and, up ahead, see a window with a frighteningly familiar glow.

It's the Blue Room, the most horrible place in the whole Horrible Place. I remember it from my nightmares. I also remember that no animal in the lab, including the guard dogs, ever wanted to go anywhere near it.

Because the Blue Room is where the Long Coats would do their dirty work. They jabbed us with needles and clipped electrodes to our heads and tails and anywhere else they wanted, no matter how painful.

The door is slightly ajar. I see a sliver of blue light leaking out.

I leap through the crack.

The guard dog won't want to follow me. He knows what goes on behind this closed door, and it isn't pretty.

Neither is what I see inside the Blue Room.

All my brothers and sisters are squirming in sealed containers stacked against the wall. They're a wiggly rainbow of glowing neon colors because of the ultraviolet light illuminating the room.

"We'll inject them one at a time," says a short man in a surgical gown. His rubber gloves glow under the black light.

"Let's start with the red one," says the tall Long Coat.

Oh, no, oh, no, oh, no.

It's Abe.

The tall Long Coat taps on a computer keyboard. "Opening container R-258."

A small light changes from red to green on the front of Abe's holding bin. The door slides open. Then the other Bad Man plucks a scared, struggling Abe out of the box by his tail!

CHAPTER 52

"Leave no mouse behind."
—Isaiah

The lab technician clutches Abe in one hand, a syringe in the other.

He's going to jab something horrible into my favorite brother.

I need to do something stupid and foolish and dangerous.

"STOP!" I shout. Humans can't hear ultrasonic sounds, but I try to make my voice deep enough to be audible. And it works!

The two humans stop what they're doing to look around the room. They're trying to figure out who's yelling at them in such a tiny voice and where it's coming from.

"LET HIM GO!" I scream.

They look down. See me.

"It's B-97!" says the short Long Coat. "The one who got away."

"Put the red one back in his box," says his partner. "Grab the blue guy."

They plop Abe back into his plastic crate. Slam it shut. The green light turns red again.

"Isaiah?" The thick walls of his plastic holding pen muffle Abe's ultrasonic voice. But I can hear it even if the humans can't. "Isaiah!"

"Welcome home!" hollers Winnie in a voice that only mice can hear.

"I thought you ran away," grunts Benji. "I thought you were a coward!"

"You thought wrong!" I tell him.

And then, using my human voice, I scream, "YOU ARE MONSTERS!" as loud as I can.

"He can speak?" says the tall Bad Man. "Wait until Dr. Ledbetter hears about this!"

The two masked men lunge at me. I dodge away from their grasps.

If they think a mouse speaking is awesome, wait until they see what I'm going to do next!

When they both miss me a second time, I hop up to that computer keyboard—the one that the tall human was tapping on. I dance across the letters as quickly as I can. Here is what I type:

open all

Every single tiny red light on the plastic holding bins blinks to green.

The prison doors pop open. My brothers and sisters hop out of their cages and scramble to the floor. All ninety-six (I did a quick head count) scamper around on the floor. The two lab technicians are trying to corral my mischief, but they forgot just how smart, fast, and clever they made us.

"Head to the back room!" I tell my brothers and sisters.

"And then what?" asks Benji.

I take a deep breath and say the word I've been teaching myself to speak ever since I first heard Mikayla sing it:

FREEDOM!

I tap-dance a few more jig steps on the keyboard. I stomp on the caps lock because, this time, I *am* screaming.

OPEN BLUE ROOM DOOR

The door flies open. My brothers and sisters zip out.

The two Long Coats don't chase after them. They're too busy marveling at me.

I distract them a little longer, hoping to give my family a head start to the back door. I keep typing.

the quick brown fox jumps over the lazy dog

"He just used twenty-six letters of the alphabet in one sentence!" says one.

I type some more:

it's called a pangram, dummies

"Trap him!" says the other.

Uh-oh.

What if I'm the only mouse who *does* get left behind?

CHAPTER 53

"Any plan is bad
if it cannot be altered."
—Isaiah

"**L**ock the door!" the two techs scream at each other.

I leap off the rolling computer stand, hit the ground at a run, and sprint for the door.

The two humans are right behind me.

I'm pumping my legs as fast as I can, but so are the two giants. One nearly steps on me!

The faster of the two lab techs lurches forward and grabs the door handle. He's pushing it shut, his thumb already on the lock button.

But there's a narrowing crack, about as wide as an envelope, as the door glides shut.

I hold my breath, suck in my gut, and squeeze through—my tail barely squeaking free before I hear the door slam behind me.

I also hear the *ka-thunk* of the lock sliding into place.

"Unlock it!" yells one of the men inside the Blue Room. "He's getting away! Unlock the door!"

Behind me, I hear the jiggle of metal as the two

technicians fumble with the lock and door handle.

The coast is clear ahead of me. I race down the hallway, hang a right, and scoot into the room near the rear exit.

Where I discover all my brothers and sisters being chased around the floor by an enraged Mr. Brophy.

CHAPTER 54

"You never fail until you quit trying."
—Isaiah

"G reat plan, Isaiah!" shouts Benji sarcastically. "Send us to a locked and bolted door! Brilliant, little brother. Brilliant!"

Mr. Brophy can't hear my big brother, but he sure can swat at Benji with his broom.

Luckily, Benji is nimble and quick. He dodges clear of the bristles just in time.

But he's right. My plan is ridiculous unless I can figure out a way to grab Mr. Brophy's keys and unlock the back door.

So I do something else I never thought I'd do. I cup my paws around my snout and shout up at Mr. Brophy. "HEY!"

Stunned, he drops his broom and crouches down to peer at me. "You're the one that got away," he says. "Why, I oughta…"

But before he can do anything, I spring off the floor and land on his bent knee.

Panicking, he starts twirling around in frantic circles and swatting himself as if he is being attacked by a swarm of bees. I hang on tight.

"Get off me, you filthy rodent!"

I pay no attention to his insult. I dig my claws into the fabric of his green work pants and haul myself up his leg until I reach his belt and the clip-on key ring.

"Need a little help!" I cry out. "Delphinia—form a tower!"

Delphinia, my purple sister, is super strong. She whistles to the other acrobats in our family, and fifteen gymnastically inclined mice quickly form a tower that climbs about two feet off the floor.

It's halfway between the door and me.

Keziah, who has better upper-body strength than anyone else in my mischief (she can bench-press a sack of sugar), is perched at the top.

I grab hold of Mr. Brophy's key ring.

"Hey!" he shrieks. "Leave that alone."

I hiss at him, something I learned from his evil cat.

Mr. Brophy's eyes nearly bug out of his head when I do that. He's frozen with fear.

"Abe? Winnie?" I shout. "Pyramid. By the door. All the way up to the lock!"

"You got it, bro!" Abe shouts back.

He and Winnie quickly organize the rest of our family into a towering mouse pyramid.

Now it's my turn to become acrobatic.

"Ready?" I shout to Keziah.

She nods, and with Delphinia anchoring the bottom, the whole ladder begins to sway, back and forth, back and forth. When they build up a little momentum, I leap off Mr. Brophy's hip and—clutching his key ring with my legs like a trapeze artist—fly through the air.

The cable attaching the keys to his belt extends freely.

Keziah grabs my front paws. She and the whole mouse tower powerfully swing me on toward the door.

I arc up. Soar toward the top of the pyramid.

I hear the cable snap. It's okay—I still have the key ring tucked under my legs. And without the retractable cable, there's nothing to slow me down or pull me backward.

I just have to trust that Abe and Winnie, poised at the top of the pyramid, will catch me.

The door is rushing right at me.

I close my eyes an instant before impact.

And feel four familiar paws grab me and hold me tight!

CHAPTER 55

"Things turn out best for the mice who make the best out of the way things turn out."
—**Isaiah**

"Dr. Ledbetter?" shouts Mr. Brophy. "Professor?" The Mop Man runs out of the room.

"We need to hurry," I say. "Dr. Ledbetter is the big cheese. He'll do anything to keep us imprisoned here."

"So many keys," says Winnie, studying the collection on Mr. Brophy's ring.

"It's this one," I say, tapping the key with the squarish black plastic head. "I watched him lock the door!"

I grab it. Abe and Winnie give me a boost, and I work the key into the keyhole.

"Got it!" I shout when the key slips into its grooves.

"Now you just have to turn it," says Abe.

I grab the side of the key with my front paws. "When I chomp into it with my teeth," I say, "take hold of my legs and jump sideways. That'll give us enough torque to twist the key!"

"Got it!" shouts Winnie.

Still clutching the key, I bite into it, too. *This has to work, it's our only chance,* I think desperately.

Abe and Winnie hold on to one of my legs, then jump off the mouse pyramid. They feel so heavy dangling from my foot, but that's the point.

Our combined weight turns the key and unlocks the door. With sheer relief I let go, and the three of us plummet to the floor. Fortunately, all the gymnast mice from Keziah's tower have scampered over to catch us.

Keziah catches me, cradling me in her arms. Delphinia one-hands Abe *and* Winnie. Our other brothers and sisters see that we're safe and tumble out of their pyramid.

"You did it!" shouts Abe.

"No," I say. "*We* did it. Hurry! We need to push the door open. Everybody, lend a shoulder."

My entire mischief, all ninety-seven of us, races to the base of the door. We all shove against it.

It won't budge.

We shove *again*.

Nothing.

"You have to pull it open," says a human voice behind us.

We whip around. It's Dr. Ledbetter. The two Blue Room technicians are with him. Mr. Brophy, too.

"I guess we didn't give you enough intelligence to figure out the difference between a door you *push* open and one you *pull*," sniggers Dr. Ledbetter. "There are only two ways to open that door. One, you can yank on the handle and pull, but I don't think any of you weigh enough to generate enough force for that to work. Two, you can have someone on the other side push it open for you. But the only person on the other side of that door is Tom, one of my best security guards."

Behind the door, I hear a pack of dogs barking.

"Well, what do you know?" sneers Dr. Ledbetter. "Sounds like Tom brought along a few of his canine friends."

Smirking, Dr. Ledbetter bends over to study me.

"It's good to see you again, B-97. My colleagues tell me that you recently demonstrated some rather unusual talents. Ones I did not know I had given you. I can't wait to open you up and see what's going on inside that tiny little blue brain of yours."

Even though the creepy doctor is talking about dissecting my skull, I don't flinch. Instead, I send an ultrasonic message to my mischief. "Step away from the door."

My brothers and sisters split down the middle and silently scurry to the sides of the exit.

Then I send out another ultrasonic signal. The battle cry Gabriel and I agreed upon: "Set the captives free!"

Outside, there's a loud screech and thunk of metal.

Apparently, while I've been busy in the lab, my mouse army figured out how to push open the tailgate at the back of Mr. Brophy's pickup truck.

And I imagine they'll have absolutely no problem pushing open an unlocked door.

CHAPTER 56

*"Sticks held together in a bundle
are unbreakable."*
—Isaiah

The dogs on the other side of the door are the first to run away.

Terrified by the overwhelming swarm of mice, they yelp and take off running.

I also hear Tom, the security guard, shriek in fear. From the disappearing sound of his cries, I gather he's running away, too.

There's a dull bang, and the steel door bulges forward at the base.

"Again!" I hear Gabriel cry.

Another rush of troops. Another bulge.

"Someone has to twist the door knob," I realize out loud. "Toss me up there, Keziah."

She grabs me under my arms and heaves me skyward like a shot put. I land on the knob, wrap my whole body around it, and give it a good twist to the right.

But nothing happens. I'm not heavy enough to make the knob turn.

As quick as lightning, my clever brothers and sisters spot the problem and come to the rescue. As they did before, Abe and Winnie leap up and grab onto my legs, giving me the weight I need to twist the knob downward.

The army outside slams into the base of the door one more time. I hang on for dear life as it nearly flies off its hinges, bursting open.

Five thousand mice pour into the room and quickly surround the four Bad Men, who are frozen in shock and fear. After all they've done to us mice, they have reason to be afraid.

There are so many brown, white, and gray mice flooding the floor, the brightly colored members of my mischief disappear completely.

I notice the smirk is completely wiped off Dr. Ledbetter's face as he recoils in terror from the sea of mice at his feet.

Then, above the squeaks of five thousand mice, there's a new voice. "You see?" shouts someone outside. "No mice? They were lying to you, officers!"

Well, hidey-ho.

Guess who just appeared at the door with a whole squadron of humans wearing dark blue uniforms?

Hailey! She spots me in the crowd. "I called 911," she says, waggling her cell phone.

I touch my paw to my heart. Since I don't have a keyboard handy, it's the only way I know to say thank you.

"Well, well, well, Dr. Ledbetter," says a woman wearing a blue windbreaker with ASPCA stenciled across the back in bright yellow letters. "You told us you didn't use any mice in your lab work."

"W-we don't," sputters Dr. Ledbetter.

"Then what do you call this?" asks a gruff, squat man. His jacket has the letters PD on the back. I don't know what ASPCA and PD mean, but I'm very glad they're here.

"This," says Dr. Ledbetter, pointing at the floor

filled with thousands of squeaking, swarming, nibbling mice, "is what I call a very serious vermin infestation. My janitorial staff was just about to call the exterminators."

"That's right," says Mr. Brophy. "I was."

"Fine," says the man with PD stenciled on his back. "That can be your one phone call. From jail."

While the humans argue and shout at one another, I decide it's time my two families escaped from the Horrible Place, once and for all.

I turn to Hailey. Give her a jaunty salute.

She salutes right back.

"See you at home," she says. "Mom bought another crumb cake."

I wiggle my eyebrows, the way my brother Rudolpho taught me.

And then I send out an ultrasonic signal that makes my heart swell with happiness. "Follow me, everybody!"

Five thousand and ninety-seven mice race out the back door, tear across the loading dock, jump off the edge, and follow my secret sewer-pipe escape route all the way to freedom.

CHAPTER 57

*"A true friend is the one who walks in
when the rest of the world walks out."*
—Isaiah

That night, in the backyard of Hailey's house,
I introduce her to my brothers and sisters.

"this is my brother and very best friend, abe,"
I type on her laptop, which she has propped open on
a picnic table.

Hailey is smiling, admiring Abe. "He's so...red!
So cool and different."

"yes," I type, "that's the only thing we all have in
common: we're all different."

Mice, of course, are very social creatures. My
brothers and sisters have already met all of Mikayla's
family, and the elders quickly declared us one big,

happy mischief. It might take a little while for my siblings to get used to their new lives and the unfamiliar burrow, but I know that they're happy and grateful to be rescued. They'll do everything they can to pull their own weight in our wonderful new mischief. And with our unique talents, there's a lot we can do to help.

After they settled in, my family wanted to meet Hailey, the nice human who helped them escape. She wanted to meet them, too.

"You're all so amazing!" Hailey says after the gymnasts in the family give her a quick display of their acrobatic skills. "I wish more people would realize how incredible you are."

I shake my head and type, "i've met many humans, and they're all the same. except you, of course."

"We just have to introduce you in a way that's not going to scare them," Hailey says. "Finding a mouse in your crumb cake can be a little surprising, you know?"

I nod, smiling.

She suddenly waves her hands excitedly, startling some of my family. "I have this great idea. No, it's better than great. It's spectacular!"

Apparently, the church she attends is having an Animal Blessing on Sunday.

"Everybody in the parish brings their pets, and the priest blesses them. It's a big celebration. You guys definitely need to be there."

"do you mean all of us?" I type.

"Okay. You're right. Hundreds of mice scurrying around the church pews might freak people out. So how about you, Mikayla, Gabriel, Abe, and Winnie?"

"do we have to dress up?" I ask, because, after all, it is church.

Hailey grins. "Maybe just a little..."

CHAPTER 58

*"Our lives may be different,
but they're also the same."*
—Isaiah

Sunday comes, and I absolutely loathe the outfit
Hailey has chosen for me.

Loathe, by the way, is a polite way of saying I HATE IT.

But I would never tell Hailey that. I am quite fond of my first human friend.

We hide in Hailey's backpack and ride with her and her parents to church.

I have never been inside a church before, but it is wonderful. When Hailey takes a seat in a pew, I peek out from under the backpack flap to study the crowd.

The church looks like a miniature version of Noah's Ark, one of my favorite biblical stories because of all the animals in it, including a pair of mice.

The churchgoers have brought all manner of pets to the special service. I see dogs in all shapes and sizes. Cats safely locked away in carriers, thank you very much. Hamsters. Guinea pigs. Rabbits. Goldfish. Parakeets. I even see a donkey and a man standing behind it with a shovel.

Hailey leans over and whispers to me. "I guess you guys want to go meet the other animals, huh?" she says.

I give her a look that says, "Can we?"

She says, "Sure. Go on. You're an animal. This is your big day."

I spy a hamster two rows down who reminds me of a distant cousin twice removed. I climb out of the backpack. Mikayla, Gabriel, Abe, and Winnie climb out right behind me.

"This is so nice," says Mikayla. "All these people love animals!"

"I guess all humans aren't like the creeps you meet in a lab," adds Abe.

The five of us scamper down the carpeted center aisle, big smiles plastered to our snouts, and BOOM!

Just like always, it happens.

"Eeeeeek! Mice! EEEEEEK!"

The shrieking. The jumping up on the seats. The usual.

Here is a church filled with animal lovers who, supposedly, want to bless and celebrate animals... and now they're going bonkers over five little mice? Sure, three of us are kind of strangely colored, but still.

It once again proves my theory that no matter how hard we try, no matter what amazing feats we perform, mice will always be outcasts in this world. I bet even Noah wasn't happy to see two of us walking up the gangplank to his ark!

Humans hate us.

Always have, always will.

CHAPTER 59

"All cats are gray in the dark."
—*Isaiah*

Hailey rushes down the center aisle, scoops us up one by one, and tucks us into her backpack.

Then, believe it or not, she walks right up to the raised podium where the human in robes was just about to speak.

"Excuse me, Father Ed, but I need to say something to the congregation. Something important."

Before Father Ed gives her permission, Hailey grabs hold of the microphone.

"Good morning, everybody. Before Father Ed blesses our animals, I want to say something about the smallest creatures among us. The ones we'll sing about later in one of my favorites hymns, 'All Things

Bright and Beautiful.' It was written way back in 1848, so maybe we've sung it so many times, we don't really hear what the words are telling us anymore. Allow me to refresh your memory."

She flips through a book filled with musical notes and starts reading.

All things bright and beautiful,
All creatures great and small,
All things wise and wonderful,
The Lord God made them all.

The crowd is silent. Even the parakeet has quit asking for a cracker.

Hailey keeps going. "Believe it or not, I've spent some time recently with some extremely great creatures who just happen to be extremely small."

She puts her hand to her shoulder and I climb on.

"This little guy is Isaiah. I've seen him do some incredible things, mostly to help his brothers and sisters. He is wise and wonderful."

She puts me down on the podium so she can give Mikayla a ride down from her backpack.

"And this brave little lady is Mikayla. She wasn't afraid to hang out with a strange-looking little blue dude like Isaiah, even though all her friends are brown, gray, or white. Why is Mikayla so kind and understanding toward others who look different?"

The priest, Father Ed, answers Hailey's question. "She's wonderful, too."

Hailey nods. "I'm different, also, if you haven't noticed. Guess what? We all are. As my wise and wonderful friend Isaiah here once told me, 'We're all different. It's the only thing we have in common.'"

The priest clears his throat. "He, uh, told you?"

"Oh, yes," Hailey says. "Isaiah can do all sorts

of incredible things. Speak. Type. Unlock doors."

Amid loud, startled whispering among the congregation, Hailey grabs the microphone and tilts it down so it's about an inch away from my whiskers.

"Come on, Isaiah. Let's show everybody how special you are."

I'm about to scream, "KIBBLE!" when Hailey prompts me: "Sing that song you told me about. The one Mikayla sang to you that night in my hoody."

I look to Mikayla.

"Go ahead," she says. "I'll help you out."

"But they won't be able to hear you. They'll barely hear *me*."

"It doesn't matter. I'll be singing for *you*, Isaiah. Just follow my lead. And this time, don't yell. Sing."

I face the microphone. Clear my throat. "Ahem."

The crowd gasps. None of them has ever heard a mouse clear his throat before.

Mikayla and I skip over the verse about mice meandering in the moonlight and jump right to the refrain:

You may tower like a giant,
You may be weak and you may be small,

Our differences make no difference,
The same moon shines on us all.

Some of the humans in the pews are starting to weep. I look at Mikayla. Her voice is so beautiful, I wish it weren't ultrasonic. Then everyone in this church could know what heaven sounds like.

"Well," says Father Ed when I'm done, "thank you, Hailey. I was going to give a sermon this morning about tolerance and loving all of God's creatures, no matter how different they may seem. But your talk was much better than anything I could have said."

The service continues. My friends and I get blessed. The donkey doesn't embarrass himself when it's his turn. All in all, it is a fantastic Sunday morning.

On the way out of church, a sweet-looking old lady leans in to Hailey and whispers, "Have fun with your singing mouse friends. But remember—they carry all sorts of germs, dear."

Hailey smiles and gives the nice lady one of my all-time favorite replies: "Maybe. But so do we."

Because, when all is said and done, none of us is very different from any of us.

EPILOGUE

After church, Abe says, "You know, Isaiah, Hailey's sermon got me thinking. If we're all God's creatures, great and small, then...all of us animals are sort of one big family, don't you think?"

"I suppose. Not that I'd want to share Thanksgiving dinner with a tiger. I'd probably *be* his dinner. Why do you ask?"

His whiskers start twitching like they do when he doesn't want to tell you something.

"What is it, Abe?" I ask.

"Well, uh, when you escaped and I was still in

the Horrible Place, I heard some of the Long Coats talking."

"And?"

"There's another Lamina Lab not too far from here, Isaiah. A place where they do stuff even *worse* than what they did to us."

I start to feel that powerful surge of injustice and indignation. More animals living in pain and terror? I want to help—I *have* to. Maybe this is what my special abilities are really for—to rescue those in need.

"You mean there are other mice in danger? Another mischief we should go rescue? Let's do it!" I say.

A few weeks ago, I was the biggest coward of my mischief. But I've learned a lot about overcoming my fears since then, especially if others' lives are at stake.

Abe shakes his head. "Not mice, but other animals. Like you said, we're all family, so they deserve to be rescued, too, right?"

I nod firmly. "Of course. No creature should be subjected to that kind of horrible life. I give you my word that we'll help them. What are they? Bunnies, guinea pigs, hamsters?"

He looks around to make sure nobody else hears

what he is about to say. "No, Isaiah. Not hamsters. *Cats.*"

YIPES!

What did I just get myself into?

I wish I could laugh and tell Abe that he's crazy. That we'd be risking our lives for cats who will gobble us up the second they're free. That they're evil creatures who would never do the same for us.

That we're *not* going to save them.

But...

I gave my word that I would help all creatures in need, great and small.

And, as you know, the word of a mouse can never be broken.

Sticks and stones
may break your bones,
but mean names
last forever!

GET A SNEAK PEEK AT

Pottymouth
and
Stoopid

AVAILABLE NOW!

The Blame Game

When you're Pottymouth and Stoopid, you get blamed for all sorts of stuff you didn't actually do.

Remember that disgusting lunch in the cafeteria?

The mystery meat in the mushy sauce on a bed of rice that might've been moving? The one everybody called "When You Find Out What It Is, Don't Tell Me"?

Well, somehow, that was our fault.

"Stoopid gave them

the recipe," went the rumor. "And Pottymouth told them to pour schnizzleflick all over it."

When the basketball team lost its first game, everybody blamed Michael.

"Pottymouth called the other team fluffer-knuckles. That's why we lost. He fired up the enemy with his pottymouthing!"

Not true, of course, but the truth seldom has anything to do with a good Pottymouth or Stoopid story.

For instance, did you know that I'm the one who opened the hamster cage in the fifth-grade classroom and set Scruffy free? Yeah, I didn't know it either. From what I heard, I saw the word *ham* on the cage. I thought there was a sandwich inside and I was hungry.

Then there was that disastrous field trip to the natural history museum. The trip when the whole *Tyrannosaurus rex* skeleton in the lobby toppled to the ground. They say I yanked out an anklebone so I could take it home to my dog.

I don't even have a dog, I told anybody who'd listen. Which would be nobody.

When Anna started hanging out with us, she got blamed for stuff too.

The power outage during the big vampire battle scene in the movie everybody was watching during study hall?

"Anna Britannica pulled the plug on the extension cord," proclaimed Kaya Kennecky. "She thought it was a bright orange Twizzler and tried to eat it."

And so it went. Day after day.

Pottymouth did this. Stoopid did that. Anna Britannica did everything else.

I realized that Michael and I had been Pottymouth and Stoopid for so long, most of the kids at school didn't know our real names.

That was okay, I guess.

Because we didn't want to know their names
either.

All Shapes and Sizes

When you think about bullies in middle school, you probably picture a gnarly mouth-breather with a huge head and a tree-stump neck.

Well, at our school, we have a pair of extremely vicious bullies: Kaya Kennecky (yep, she hasn't changed a bit since pre-K) and Tiffany Blurke.

BULLYUS TYPICALLUS

That's right. They're both girls, not muscle-
bound boys.

Day in and day out, those two girls picked on
Anna Brittoni without mercy. Most of the junk
they pulled took place during gym class. They
hid her school clothes so she had to go to class in
stinky workout gear. They poured baby oil on the
floor in front of her locker. They filled her backpack with shaving cream. They stole her Snickers
bar and refilled the wrapper with wet newspaper.

Then one day in the cafeteria, Kaya and Tiffany went too far.

When Anna wasn't looking, they snatched her most prized possession—her basketball scorebook—and sent it down the dirty-tray line. It was like running a paperback book through a car wash without a car. The thing was soaked, trashed, mangled, and mashed.

Anna had spent hours recording every single shot of every single game in that book. Now the pages were all glued together and covered with smushed lima beans.

Of course, Kaya and Tiffany denied everything.

"She did it herself," they whined to Mrs. Rattner, who was on cafeteria duty that day. "She left it on her tray accidentally on purpose just so she could blame us."

Anna was furious but she didn't show it. She just went back to class and kept scoring 100s and getting A-pluses on everything the school threw at her.

But Michael and I knew Anna was really hurt.

We also knew that she'd just learned what

we'd learned a long time ago: Fly under the radar. Keep a low profile. That way, you make yourself a smaller target.

"If you stay invisible," said Michael, "it's harder for the sniffefligly flufferknuckles to take shots at you."

Anna had a saying of her own: "Revenge is a dish best served cold."

At first, I thought she was talking about the corn dogs in the cafeteria because they're like fake-meat Popsicles wrapped in pre-chewed Fritos.

But a few days after the "incident" with Anna's scorebook, there was another "incident." One that everybody talked about for weeks.

Because it happened to two of the school's prettiest, most popular people.

Kaya and Tiffany.

How to Get Even

At first, Michael and I wondered why Anna would come to school with a roll of plastic wrap.

Was it for some kind of science experiment about osmosis or nonporous surfaces?

Was she wrapping sandwiches in one of her classes? If so, how lame was *that* class?

"Maybe she's just gone hyper-clean," said Michael. "She wants to wrap all her pens, pencils, and junk in plastic to keep 'em sterile. Maybe, with enough plastic wrap, she can seal out the grizzlegoop germs that cause bad breath too."

Then we heard about the "unfortunate incident" in the girls' locker room.

It seems somebody stretched a sheet of clear plastic across both of the toilet seats right before Kaya and Tiffany went into the stalls. Of course Kaya and Tiffany were always the first ones to use the two toilets right after gym class. None of the other girls were allowed to relieve themselves until after the big two did number one.

Funny thing about plastic wrap. If you stretch it tight enough across a toilet, it sort of becomes invisible. Especially when the toilet seat is down, and when it comes to bathrooms, girls always want the toilet seat down (or so my mom tells me on a regular basis).

Anyway, there was, shall we say, a problem. Kaya and Tiffany both ended up with gym shorts that became used diapers. Within an hour, their accident in the girls' locker room turned into the "unfortunate incident."

Anna confessed to the crime.

"Call it revenge," she told the vice principal.

Presenting: The Princess and the Pee

"Therefore, it was served cold."

She was sent home immediately—but not before she donated the rest of her plastic wrap to the cafeteria. "Use it for the leftover corn dogs," she told them. "It'll stop them from tasting like whatever you keep in your freezer that you probably shouldn't."

Principal Ferguson and Vice Principal Driscoll gave Anna only a half-day suspension. She was instructed to report back to school the very next morning because that's when we'd be taking some more state tests. If Anna didn't take them, the average score at our school would probably drop by three points.

Yeah, Anna Britannica is *that* smart.

Anyway, after that we were treated to an afternoon filled with serious discussions.

"We need to talk about this, kids," said Ms. Funkleberger, our social studies teacher, who everybody said was a real-life hippie. "What Anna did was soooo wrong."

Ms. Funkleberger was probably sixty-something years old with frizzy hair and granny glasses tinted pink. Most of her clothes were tie-dyed.

"So let's rap," she said to the class. "Let it all hang out."

"Why did Anna have to be so mean to poor Kaya and Tiffany?" this one girl asked. "What'd they ever do to her?"

Plenty, I wanted to say. But I didn't. Because I fly under the radar, remember?

"I don't get it," said a guy. "It's crazy. *She's* crazy."

"That Anna girl is weird," said another girl, a friend of Kaya's. "She writes a million numbers in a notebook during every single basketball game. I'm sorry, but that is a sign of a true wackadoodle weirdo."

Yeah, most of the other kids in Ms. Funkleberger's class couldn't understand why anybody would play such a mean trick on sweet Kaya and Tiffany.

Michael and me?

We totally got it.

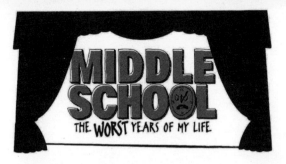

JAMES PATTERSON

**To find out more about James Patterson
and his bestselling books, go to
www.jamespatterson.co.uk**